PRAISE FOR CROW'S REST:
FAERIE CROSSED BOOK 1

"The story has a timeless quality about it, mixed with a connection to history, mythology, and fairy tales, and it includes themes of magic, romance, friendship, and family. Jackson has delightful and often flirty humor woven into a story of courage, adventure, love, secrets, and strength."

– SAN FRANCISCO BOOK REVIEW

PRAISE FOR MERLIN'S STRONGHOLD:
FAERIE CROSSED BOOK 2

"This fast-paced and smooth-flowing story will have readers holding onto the edge of their seats throughout, with lots of thrilling suspense, wicked magic and witty dialogue. The characters are strong and compelling, with the heroine having a fun, snarky attitude that will delight readers and make them chuckle."

– E.L HURLEY, InD'tale Magazine

SPELLMEET

FAERIE CROSSED
BOOK 3

ANGELICA R. JACKSON

Crow & Pitcher Press
SHINGLE SPRINGS, CA

For permission requests, write to the publisher at: Crow & Pitcher Press, P.O. Box 1294, Shingle Springs, CA 95682
www.CrowAndPitcherPress.com

Book Layout ©2017 BookDesignTemplates.com
Interior mountain illustration via Shutterstock
Interior design by Angelica R. Jackson
Cover design & photo manipulation by Kelley York of Sleepy Fox Studio, using artwork by Angelica R. Jackson

Spellmeet/ Angelica R. Jackson -- 1st ed.
ISBN 978-0-9987214-7-7
Library of Congress Control Number: 2022938942

*For all the Hounds and moggies who grace us
with their spirits*

Books by Angelica R. Jackson:

Faerie Crossed Series

Crow's Rest
Merlin's Stronghold
Spellmeet

Non-Fiction
Capturing the Castle:
Images of Preston Castle (2006-2016)

1 Avery

You'd think that ruling Faerie for however-many thousands of years would have earned you a happily ever after. Or at least a retirement party with all your office frenemies raising a glass to you and singing a round of "For She's a Jolly Good Fae Queen" while you pretend to smile.

But Queen Maeve didn't get a gold watch and vague invitations to "do lunch sometime." Instead, she was spending her last days in the care home where Lonan and I worked, a royal Fae fitting right in with the frail and damaged humans.

The queen had ended up there by trusting me with her magic, which I'd then lost. Well, technically, I gave her magic to Uncle Tam so I could get my own wild magic back—before I lost that too (and Uncle Tam died).

Whatever you wanted to call it, the end (or the end-of-the-world) result was the same: Queen Maeve found herself powerless, throneless, friendless, and homeless. Without a ruler, the other royal Fae decided a civil war was the best way to find a replacement. One particularly brutal family would take over the Court, only to be displaced—dismembered—by an even more vicious tribe. It turned out that without a monarch to keep them in line, the Fae were just as self-destructive as humans.

Except, now the humans were more united than they'd ever been in history. Apparently having a border blow up between your world and one that most people hadn't believed existed, and then having a psycho wild magician try to burn every living thing on his funeral pyre, will do that. In the less-impacted regions, the human Faerie-deniers didn't believe that was what really happened, and blamed government experiments instead.

It was harder to believe it was a hoax if you were one of the humans who woke up to find a chunk of Faerie—like a dark forest or a life-sized gingerbread castle—literally dropped into your backyard. If you chose to stay, you could look forward to new experiences like dead gnomes left on the doormat by your cat. Or, you know, your cat getting eaten by Fae neighbors.

On the flip side, social media was aghast with the long list of people and places missing from the worlds. All anyone knew was that it was like the residents of random towns had been raptured or abducted by aliens, along with beloved landmarks—leaving Faerie and the human world as smaller and lesser lands.

Let's just say it was an adjustment after what came to be called the Shifting, and it would be for years to come.

If I hadn't joined my powers with Merlin's and given him the chance to enact his villainous plans in the first place, our worlds would still be intact. Sure, I'd tried to stop him, and to save as much as I could from burning with him. But with the queen's powers in my hands—the mantle of royal magic the Sovereign carried—I should have been able to do more, right? At least that's what I beat myself up with on a daily basis.

The thing was, every single person in Faerie and the human world would have gladly beaten me up for those same crimes. As far as they were concerned, Avery Flynn alone was responsible for all of it: the destruction as the failing border devoured their homes and families, my betrayal of Queen Maeve, and the feral pockets of magic that made spells or technology unstable in the twisted ruins now called Spellmeet.

On my bad days, I agreed with them and the dark thoughts crushed me. Paralyzed me. But on my better days, I knew Merlin would have kept trying to breed another wild magic baby. I wasn't even his first attempt—just the first one powerful enough (and trusting enough) to fuel his funeral pyre.

If it hadn't been me, then maybe some other person would have faced off with Merlin, and if they hadn't been as persistent—okay, as stubborn and bossy—as I was, we'd be even worse off now. As in, *nobody* would be alive to care or point fingers at me.

Surprisingly, Queen Maeve herself didn't blame me for her circumstances. But I genuinely didn't know if it was because she really was that forgiving, or because she didn't remember all the details. Lately, the erosion of her memory and her body had been accelerating. "Erosion" was not just a specific word choice; she was physically crumbling away.

It started as a few grains of sand among the sheets, like she'd climbed into bed without washing her feet after a walk on the beach. Then there was the morning when I went to change her bed and there were two piles of sand where her feet used to be.

The loss of her feet didn't seem to cause her any pain, and it confused her if I tried to talk to her about it or ask her if we could fix them. *How—with concrete or spackle? That fake stone they make kitchen countertops out of or something?* She wasn't lucid enough to explain to me what was happening.

Lonan was a better source of Fae info, and he said that as an oread, a Fae associated with mountains and morphology, it wasn't completely unexpected she would deteriorate like this.

"You mean this is normal for her?" I asked. "All oreads eventually fall into sand?"

He rubbed his hand over his hair like it was still a long, feathery mane (even though he'd had short hair for a long time now) before he answered. "Well, not normal...but not unheard of either. Normal for oreads is for them to end their lives by joining with their mountain, after a looooong, long lifetime. They sort of move less and less until you realize they haven't moved in thousands of years and that rock outcrop looks just like Great-Uncle Galtymore."

"We need to take your aunt to her mountain then? Do you know where it is in Faerie?"

He hesitated again, and I recognized his expression of "if I tell you this, it'll make you feel bad..."

and I crossed my arms. Glared at him until he sighed and continued.

"It was destroyed with Merlin, when time ran out for you to move things to save them. Her mountain didn't make the crossing."

I sat heavily on the chair next to Maeve's bed. I'd had nightmares every night about the people and things that didn't make it safely out of Merlin's pyre, but I tried to avoid thinking about them during the day. Otherwise, I'd be too overwhelmed to actually do anything else—and really, what could I do but try to make up for it?

Lonan's touch on my shoulder snapped me back to Maeve's room. I reached up to hold his hand and nodded, bracing myself for more difficult words.

"If we can't do anything to fix it, is she in pain? Can she feel this happening to her?"

"I don't think so," he said softly. "The sand, it's because of the magic leaving her. She would normally go back to her mountain to recharge, so to speak, but without that option the magic is just seeping away. You could say the mountain was what was holding her together..."

I sighed. "So that's it. We keep her comfortable while she crumbles."

Lonan started to say something more, but he was interrupted by shouting from down the corridor and we both had to go see if we needed to help.

Chaos met us in the common room as Mr. Smith, one of the residents, hollered about tiny people stealing his shoelaces to keep him from leaving. The tiny people—sprites—did take them, but they were on the payroll for exactly that job.

Mr. Smith probably would have been put in a mental facility before the border disaster, because of his inability to distinguish between reality and his own hallucinations, but now he was just one of the survivors taking refuge at Shady Grove Home. All we'd been able to piece together was that he'd gone into Faerie when the border was down, looking for his kids who had disappeared. He had reappeared later in Spellmeet, without his kids but with whatever experience that haunted him playing on a permanent loop in his head.

Medications helped keep him subdued and something like happy, but we had given up other forms of therapy that might help him remember what had happened. They'd only made him worse, and he'd begged us not to make him relive it any more than he already did.

Shady Grove Home was a former memory-care facility so it was a good set up for housing people who might wander off looking for missing loved ones. The building had lots of windows so residents could watch the garden and pond, plus magicked hallways that dumped you back in the common room without an employee's warding badge. A neat, if improvised, solution to the problem of traumatized survivors.

With everything handled for now, Lonan and I headed to Mrs. Shore's office to clock out. The morning with Queen Maeve and Mr. Smith had left me pensive.

"Hey, do you ever wonder if there is a place like this full of orphans somewhere?" I asked. "Maybe we could bring some of them here and these people could find some healing. You know, find some family."

"You mean make them think they were reunited with their dead and missing family members?"

I winced; Lonan still occasionally thought like a Fae, even though he spent nearly all his time around humans these days. "No, I meant that even though it wouldn't be the same as getting their family back, they could comfort each other. Like how everyone at Shady Grove has become our family, now that we're cut off from everyone and everything we knew before."

Since so many people and creatures wanted us dead, I couldn't have any contact with my parents. That wasn't such a hardship with my dad since we hadn't reconciled before I had to disappear, but I missed my mom a lot. But my missing her wasn't worth putting her in danger; if anyone thought she knew where I was, there were a lot of horrible ways they could make her tell them. So it was better she didn't even know if I was alive or not, right?

Lonan's royal blood meant a faction of Fae was willing to overlook his "crimes" in favor of putting the queen's nephew on the throne. He was dodging them as much as the ones who wanted him to pay for his association with me, and he only occasionally snuck into Faerie.

Sneaking into Merlin's old housetree to raid his magical pantry was one of those times, because stocking Shady Grove's fridge and freezer saved the home a lot of money we could use to better care for the patients. (It was only a side benefit that I personally got to eat a lot of lasagna from a now-defunct restaurant, since it was magically preserved in Merlin's pantry.) But since the care home had a regular freezer, not one magicked to be bottomless, we'd just about depleted supplies from our last trip and he was going to have to go again.

When we were in bed that night, I wrapped him tightly in my arms.

"Avery? What's up?" Lonan asked with a slight wheeze since I was squeezing him.

"I'm worried about this trip tomorrow. You know you don't have to go get food, right? Shady Grove managed to budget for food before and we can do it again."

"No, I don't have to go. But it's foolish to let all that food sit there, and we're the only ones who know about it. We may as well take advantage of it."

"But it's the only place you go to regularly," I argued. "What if someone notices a pattern and is waiting for you tomorrow? Not being predictable is Outlaw 101."

He laughed and squeezed me back. "I mastered my outlaw skills years long before you were born, Avery Girl. I think I can handle myself."

"Patronize me again and you will be handling yourself in the future," I grumbled as I tried to disengage from his body.

But he held me tight and covered my face in kisses, making me squirm. "Eww, stop being so mushy—" I stopped talking because I'd brushed up against a body part which was definitely not mushy. He waggled his eyebrows suggestively.

"You just reminded me how ancient you are," I said. "I'm not in the mood now."

But I couldn't say it with a straight face, and Lonan took that as permission to roll me onto my back and kiss me in earnest. Plus he did some other distracting things which made me forget my worries for a few hours.

The next morning, he left on his trip as scheduled. He would drive to the edge of Spellmeet and then cross into Faerie, at which point he would be able to use magic to travel and haul back the food in his bottomless knapsack.

Security was much tighter on the return crossing to Spellmeet from Faerie; if you were foolish enough to sneak into Faerie, the authorities saw that as a way to Darwin out the stupid ones from the population. But humans didn't necessarily want every Tam, Puck, and Fairy coming into Spellmeet so there were checkpoints spaced along its perimeter.

So far, Lonan's cloaking spell had held up, but if a guard with the Sight saw through his glamour, they might also recognize him as a wanted Fae. They weren't as likely to kill him on sight as most Fae would, but taking him prisoner would make things way more complicated.

So when Lonan was an hour late getting home, I was beyond worried. By the time a car pulled up, I ran out to the driveway, ready to tear into him for taking so long. And then smother him with kisses for coming back safely.

That was when I noticed he wasn't driving his car. Instead of an old, silver Nissan Sentra, this was a glossy black muscle car with gleaming chrome. At least, that was what Nykur usually looked like when he shape-changed to his perfect car form, but this time he had a jagged scrape on the hood.

As I stroked a hand along the path of the missing paint, the chassis shuddered.

"What is this from? Did you get in a fight?" I asked Nykur.

An exhalation of steam answered me, enough like a sigh to recognize it.

"Let's get the food unloaded and then we can all talk," Lonan said.

Nykur's trunk popped open, and it took several trips to carry all the stuff inside. On the last trip, man-form Nykur followed us, holding the remaining trays of lasagna. He let me get a look at the scar across his cheek; raised and reddened, it simultaneously looked fresh and old, like a keloid.

"Is that from an enchanted dagger?" I asked as I found room for the trays in the freezer. "Don't the Host use those?"

"I had to go to Court so I could search for something. As soon as I found it, I tried to leave, but one of the Host tried to stop me. He gave me this wound while I was choking him to death."

I gaped at the stark confession.

"I know how that sounds," he said. "But I promise you it will be worth it. This is our chance to fix things before all the royal Fae kill each other off."

"What is?" I asked.

In answer, he reached into his jacket and pulled out something sparkly. It was a necklace, worked in some Fae metal and set with stones. The stones, blood-red ringed in white, looked exactly like if you had taken a cross section of a bone while the marrow was alive. Even without magic of my own, my Sight still worked, and that necklace set off all kinds of alarms.

"What is it?" I asked.

"These stones—they're the remnants of Queen Maeve's mountain. They're the last of her magic."

2 Brynn

"Are you a real Faerie princess?" a small voice asked.

Brynn could not locate the whisper, until a light touch on her slippers followed. Pretending to fumble her napkin, Brynn bent to peer under the table.

"Indeed I am," she answered in a low voice. "Are you a human child?"

In the dim light filtering through the hanging cloth, teeth flashed white as the creature grinned. "Of course I am. Haven't you seen a kid before?"

"Is that surprising, if you have never seen a real princess of Faerie? I have not been to your world before, and my family does not admix with humans."

"Oh. My family's dead." As younglings often do, she suddenly changed the subject and asked, "Are your parents king and queen? You're magic, right? Do you have a unicorn? I want to see a unicorn."

Brynn stifled a laugh at the flurry of questions and sat up, to see if anyone had noticed her absence. The other diners seemed unaware of her underground conversation—save for Brynn's mother, Lady Massif, who gritted her teeth across from her. But if Lady Massif had known a human was that near, she would have screeched the walls down, so she was likely only judging Brynn's fumbling with her napkin.

A human in one corner of the room then caught Brynn's eye; she was unobtrusively sliding her foot under the tables lining the wall, probing beneath them for something. An errant child, perhaps? When the young woman made eye contact with her, Brynn delicately inclined her chin and raised her eyebrows. A frown crossed the human's features before she sighed and gave Brynn a strained smile.

Did Brynn dare to help the human reclaim the child? Her instincts told her it would be the right thing to do, but then her instincts had been nearly beaten out of her on several occasions. *Only nearly, however.*

Brynn raised her wine glass and took a sip—it was sour and grainy, nothing like Fae wine—and as she set it down, she deliberately tipped the glass towards her mother's fine dress. The flurry of shrieks and apologies—a human servant actually touched her lady mother in an attempt to blot the stains!—gave the human time to pull a small, reluctant form from underneath the table and out the door without anyone besides Brynn noticing. Disaster averted.

But now it was not only her mother who judged her: a lord further down the table curled a lip in her direction, showing rows of sharp teeth, and Brynn shrank into her chair. She would never get used to—but that was not correct, she would have to get used to such obvious threats. After all, she was marrying a wyvern.

A wyvern who was every bit as crass, loud, and intimidating as the rest of his kind, but who had profited from the border's fall by trading with humans in Spellmeet. His family's fortune made her own parents willing to overlook this moral failure, in favor of an alliance between their children.

To their relief, Lord and Lady Massif would only be expected to come to Spellmeet for this betrothal banquet—the ceremony itself would be held in Faerie. They would not have to sully their shoes with the grime of so many humans ever again, once they had surrendered their daughter to her scaled groom.

After the wedding, Brynn was unlikely to see much outside of Spellmeet—except for trips back to her mountain to recharge her magic, of course. Not even the basest of husbands would deny those pilgrimages, unless he wanted the slow death of his wife. Which, who knew, with wyverns…

She tried, but failed, to suppress a shudder at the memory of touring Phoenix's family home that morning. She had hoped married life would bring an improvement in her circumstances, but the cloistered chambers awaiting her were on a par with the tower room she would be leaving behind in her family's castle.

She dropped her hands into her lap to hide their wringing, but realized she had spilled much of the wine on her skirts, when she had only intended to distract her mother with the "accident." With a sigh, she turned to the side as she stood, hoping Lady Massif would not notice the bloom of red on her outfit as she left the table.

Alas, it was an unanswered hope.

"Daughter, you are an embarrassment," Lady Massif hissed. "Go get cleaned up before your bridegroom sees you in such a state—"

"Is there something wrong, my lady?" Phoenix called down the table. He had left her side to speak with a business associate an hour before and not returned, to her relief.

Brynn's shoulders hunched involuntarily under her fiance's judgmental gaze. His polite request sounded menacing, and turned her mother into a simpering toady.

"Nothing to concern yourself with, my lord. My daughter would like to go change her clothing..."

She trailed off as her future son-in-law waved to the nearest human and ordered them to see to Lady Brynn. It happened to be the human who had retrieved the child from under the table, so Brynn went with her willingly enough. Here was a chance to get some of her curiosity answered.

As they entered a long dark hallway at the back of the restaurant, Brynn noticed the human watching her from beneath a flop of blue hair. Her black clothes were tidy, but tattoos peeping from the sleeve cuffs and the barely tamed hairdo hinted at a wilder side to this human.

"You did not punish the child too harshly, I hope?" Brynn asked.

Startled dark eyes turned to her, before the human answered, "No, she did not do any real harm.

She was more in danger from—" she broke off mid-sentence.

"From my kind, yes?"

The human did not answer, and ushered Brynn into a cluttered room. A rack of clothing took up an entire corner, and a battered sofa held the sleeping form of the child. A tatty blanket covered her, but at least it showed some care for her welfare.

The human waited for Brynn to look back to her before she asked, "Would you like to see if we can clean that dress, or do you want to see if there's something else to fit you, my lady?"

"Please call me Brynn," she answered as she came to look closer at the rack of clothes. "What is your name?"

"I'm Mara."

"And the child?"

"That's Riley." Mara's brow furrowed, and she subtly shifted her footing so she was between Brynn and the sleeping girl.

Brynn could not blame her; Fae fixations on human children rarely ended well for the child. She smiled and said, "Do not worry. I did not want her punished any more than you do."

The clothes on the rack were odd—many different styles and sizes, and some with a strange smell attached to them. To her aural sense, others bore the echo of some former spell. "I am not sure if any-thing here is suitable for my lord's standards. Why do you not have staff to cast a spell to clean these, or to glamour them?"

"Magic is sketchy here in Spellmeet, so we try not to use it for little things. Do you need help get-ting out of your dress?"

Brynn raised her eyebrows, startled into blurt-ing, "Are you—is that an overture? I cannot tell." Her mother had warned her of the human appetite for Fae partners.

Mara flashed a grin and Brynn got a sense of her true nature in that moment. Wicked delight and playfulness in those eyes.

But the human swallowed whatever cheeky re-ply she might have made and said, "Not at the mo-ment; your dress might be easier to clean if it's off. I'm offering my help so you can get back to your fiancé."

Brynn's own playfulness dwindled at the re-minder she would be returning to the celebration. "Yes. If you could help me with my laces, please."

Mara went silent as she concentrated on undoing the knot at the back of Brynn's dress, and Brynn suppressed a shiver as the girl's breath heated the nape of her neck. The weight of the silk overdress falling from her body was a relief, and Brynn stepped out of the folds, wearing only a lightweight chemise.

Mara shook out the dress and looked more closely at the stain. "Feel free to sit down," she said, distracted.

Brynn looked around and chose a plush bench in front of the lighted vanity, but as she took a seat she was startled by a tentacular creature reaching for her with a snarl. It was hairy and multicolored, in hues of purple, and altogether strange. Brynn reached a hand towards it, and it came alive with evil intent as it reached back.

Mara warned, "That thing does not play nice with strangers."

"What is it?"

"It used to be my friend Austin's party wig, until some Fae jokester thought it would be funny to enchant it. It nearly strangled Austin before we got it off him. Now it lives on that hook, and eats moths— which is good for the clothes stored in here. But otherwise a pain in the ass."

Its magic struck her aural senses like the cries of young bloodbirds, making Brynn's magic rise. "It does not seem happy with its lot. Shall I fix it?"

"Hmm?" Mara looked up from blotting the wine stain with a cloth. "I wouldn't bother—"

She broke off as the writhing creature stilled under Brynn's touch. It no longer sent out jarring notes to Brynn's ears, instead it rang harmoniously along with the other things in the room. Now it was only hanging strands of brightly colored synthetic hair, as it should be.

Mara sighed and said, "Thanks for trying, but no one has been able to fix it for long. It always comes back, meaner than ever."

But Brynn smiled and petted the wig. "It will not bother you now. The enchantment has been removed and its true nature restored."

"I wish." Mara snorted and Brynn turned, eyes wide at the sound.

"Seriously, I've called in favors to get that thing exorcised and nothing sticks," Mara continued. "It's evil."

"Not evil, merely enchanted. Or at least it was."

Mara eyed her skeptically before picking up a broom and poking the strands with the handle. "What makes you so sure?"

"Because I am a carreg." At Mara's blank look, she added, "You are not familiar with the term carreg? What about oreads?"

"The queen was an oread, right? Oreads are like mountain Fae, I think. Not, like mountain Fae, like they wear animal furs and smell like a bear. But their magic is something to do with mountains?"

Brynn tried to figure out what furs and smelling like a bear might have to do with it, but gave up and forged on. "We do have a connection to our mountains, as dryads do with trees. But oread magic is to do with restoring balance in the world—or worlds. Helping to make order out of chaos. We carregs are oreads who can sense wrongness even more deeply via the aural plane."

"I'm still not getting it." Mara looked back to the quiescent wig. "What is an aural plane? And you're saying a chaos spell was used on that wig?"

"An aural plane is a…dimension beyond how most Fae sense magic. And the wig was not affected by chaos, precisely. It was more a case of an enchantment being imposed upon its true nature, and order helps it be itself again."

"Your magic helps it be itself again," Mara said slowly. "So it will be normal from now on? No strangling tentacles or moth eating?"

"From what I understand of your moths, it is now in more danger of moths getting entangled in it."

"Hmm." Mara went back to blotting the silk dress, shooting occasional glances at the hairpiece. She did not ask any more questions about carreg magic, but her furrowed brow showed she must still be thinking through the lore Brynn had shared.

Brynn amused herself by opening the pots of cosmetics on the vanity and giving them a sniff. She could not resist dipping a finger into a silvery-blue powder and experimentally rubbing it on the back of her hand.

"Brynn?" Mara's voice made Brynn start guiltily. She had not asked before trying the powder, and such an intrusion on her mother's belongings would have earned a swift punishment.

"Yes?" she asked, hiding her hand in her lap.

Mara did not continue right away. She seemed to be choosing her words carefully before she asked, "Do you want to marry Phoenix? It's just that you seem to be afraid of him. Not that I blame you, because he and his family can be total di—divas."

It did not sound like that was her intended word for Phoenix's family, but Brynn could understand why Mara wanted to be circumspect. Wyverns were notoriously touchy and unforgiving. But would they also use a human to spy on her? To trick her into saying something they could then use against her?

Now it was Brynn's turn to be choosy with her words. "It is a good match for our families. And I can be helpful to Phoenix's business enterprises."

Mara snorted again. "I bet you can, if you're able to remove enchantments. But is it what you want? To spend your long life with him?"

Brynn could not quite suppress her wince before it showed. Mara nodded knowingly and came to stand by Brynn's bench.

"You know you don't have to marry him, right? Especially with your Carrie powers."

"Carreg," she corrected. "But my powers are not especially valued, nor are they particularly useful. The other Fae resent us for meddling with their spells and glamour. I was not even invited to debut at Court, lest I cause trouble there. My parents did not bother to give me a proper mountain name— Brynn means hill. That was how small I was to them."

"But that's in Faerie—it's different here in Spellmeet. Since the border destructed, magic takes on a life of its own here. Wild magic runs—well, wild— and screws everything up. Even human things and technology are affected. I have a freakin' singing toaster at home that won't shut up, and burns my toast too. You could totally fix it for me, right? I can put up with the toast burning, but not the singing."

"I could likely fix it, yes, as long as it is not wild magic causing the trouble. If the wild magic is pure, there is nothing I can do, but most of the wild magic here in this restaurant is mixed with more traditional Fae magic. That I can fix.

"So you believe that is why Phoenix's family approached mine with an offer of marriage? We were puzzled at first on why they want me, but he explained I am to help him gain an advantage over his business rivals with my talents."

Mara scoffed. "But that's what I'm saying—why should you use your carreg magic for his benefit, when you can use it for yours? It could be your ticket out of this marriage, if you really don't want to go through with it. You could make a killing in Spellmeet with the ability to undo enchantments."

Mara went to look again at the rack of clothing to hide her conflicting emotions. She picked out a satin corset and an incongruous lacy skirt, both in stark black and suitable for the trepidation she felt about getting married.

As she stepped behind a screen to put them on, she thought, *Could it be true? Could I truly make a break from my family's scorn and overbearing ways?*

She suspected marrying Phoenix would only be trading one autocratic family for another. As bad as her mother was, Brynn had sensed Phoenix's punishments could be worse. If she defied him in this, would he wash his hands of her or make her sorry for it?

Even in the best-case scenario where her family and Phoenix's left her alone, it would mean she was *alone*. Where would she even live? At her mountain, or Spellmeet, or somewhere she had never even been before? The prospects were both thrilling and frightening.

It would be easier to keep to her betrothal, where she would likely have the same sort of small life she had known. *Unless you make a mistake and Phoenix's punishments are worse than those you have known...* a voice whispered in her head. Brynn caught herself curling protectively over her gut, the memory of her mother's pointed shoes making contact still fresh from some infraction years ago.

At least she had learned to predict her mother's outbursts—but there would surely be a learning curve for a wyvern husband. If she felt some affection for Phoenix, it might be worth the risk. But when she felt only nervousness about him, edging into outright fear? It was not the love match she had fantasized about as a child. Phoenix was not the lover who would stand up to Brynn's family and insist she had value.

Brynn caught herself shaking her head as she faced Mara and said, "You are correct that I do not want to wed Phoenix. But I do not know where to even begin to separate from my family and their plans for me; I have nothing of my own, and I want nothing of theirs."

Mara patted her arm. "That makes it easier. You can slip out the back door and they won't have a clue where to look for you. You can make a fresh start on your own terms."

Brynn searched the girl's eyes, looking for some sign of mockery or mischief. But although this Mara had shown she was capable of wicked looks, for now she only expressed encouragement and open curiosity.

"You make it sound simple," Brynn sighed. "I am not sure I can be that brave."

"Hey, you helped me out with Riley, even though it made things harder for you at the table. Maybe you've never had to test out how brave you are yet. Aren't you curious to see?"

Maybe because she had heard her name spoken, Riley sat up on the couch and yawned hugely. "Mara, when are we—hey, you're the Faerie princess. I recognize your shoes, your Gracity."

Your Gracity? Brynn stifled a chuckle and said solemnly, "Yes, I am she, Human Child."

Riley squinted at her and asked, "What happened to your dress? And why are you wearing a

Goff tutu instead? Is it what Faerie princesses wear?"

Brynn raised an enquiring eyebrow and Mara said, "She means Goth—like dark, morbid clothing. Not a bad thing, in my book."

Mara had a book of morbid clothing? Unless it was a figure of speech; it was twice as hard to figure out idioms when two humans were speaking.

"I chose this garb only a moment ago," Brynn explained with a smile. "So I suppose it is what Faerie ladies wear. Although my family is royal, I am not a princess."

"Okay." Riley bounced to her feet. "Mara, when are we going to leave? And can Her Gracity come for a sleepover?"

Mara's smile thinned with tension. "Well, Brynn might be leaving with us, but I don't think she can come to stay..."

She trailed off, leaving room for Brynn to speak up. But Brynn had not actually decided on a plan yet, so she merely gazed back.

"Where do you live then?" Riley asked. "Maybe I can sleep over at your house sometime? Ooo, do you know how to make unicorn cupcakes? They're my favorite."

Unicorns again! Brynn laughed and answered, "I do not yet have a place to live." And with that "yet," she knew she had made a decision after all. She was going to leave her parents and fiancé behind tonight.

"Mara can help you find one!" the child squealed. "She knows everyone and every place. Right, Mara?"

At first, Mara did not look like she appreciated being nominated as house hunter, but then that wicked gleam came back into her eyes. "Oh yeah, I know the perfect place for Brynn. Mrs. Dibbs is going to love her."

With a whoop, Riley galloped from the room. Brynn hesitated before following and Mara asked if she wanted to take the dress after all.

"No," Brynn answered, "none of that was ever mine."

3 Brynn

As they left the room, Brynn took a moment to pull the quiescent wig from its hook and tuck it under her arm. Mara and Riley led the way by tip-toeing out the back door of the premises, and Brynn found herself in a dimly lit alley.

Her companions put their belongings in the back of an odd chariot, one with a single wheel in front and a patched canopy over a bench in back, over two spoked wheels. There was no yoke for an animal, and it did not have the unpleasant stench of grease and burning that the combustion vehicles did. Brynn had always been fascinated by the bits of human technology she had come across, but nothing so large as a vehicle had ever been close enough for her to examine it.

"Do you want to ride or pedal?" Mara asked.

Brynn looked up from her inspection and was about to explain she did not know what that meant, when she saw the mischievous glint in Mara's eyes once again.

"Don't worry, we'll put this ride on account," Mara continued. "Hop in back with Riley."

Brynn gingerly climbed up beside the girl and watched how Mara put her foot to one of a pair of levers. She pushed off the ground and the levers rotated, moving the wheels. *Or did the levers move the looped chain, which in turn moved the wheels..?*

"This is ingenious!" Brynn exclaimed. "Did you design this vehicle yourself?"

Riley seemed to think it was hilarious that Brynn was so impressed by their transport. "It's only a rickshaw, Princess Brynn! Don't you have them in Faerie?"

Brynn's cheeks heated a little for being laughed at by a child, but it did not seem too mean-spirited.

"No, we do not, but I did have an indentured unicorn to pull my carriage when I was a child. Does that top a rickshaw?"

Now Riley's eyes were as big as dragon scales and her mouth opened and closed soundlessly, until she let out a screech that made Mara wobble the front wheel in startlement.

"Really a unicorn? Tell me all about it. Were you friends and do they really smell like marshmallow cereal?" A thousand other questions followed until she had to take a gasping breath.

"Now you've done it," Mara said, slightly out of breath herself from moving the rickshaw. "You won't get her to shut up until she's ferreted out every last unicorn detail."

Brynn was happy to oblige, though most of the cheerful adventures she shared with Riley were made up on the spot. She sensed the child did not want to hear that Sparklewhisp was actually a curmudgeon of a unicorn, resentful that his indenture sentence was to drag around a useless carreg. He had bitten her hard enough to leave a scar on more than one occasion. And Brynn did not know what marshmallow cereal smelled like, but Sparklewhisp himself most often smelled like the skunk cabbage leaves he smoked in his pipe.

Mara took them through streets bustling with people and Fae, each going about their business. Some of the buildings still showed heavy damage but new residents had stretched canvas or boards across gaps and made them livable again. Dingy walls displayed cheeky phrases painted or scratched into their surfaces:

Got wood? Don't knock dryads!

Beware of the brownie, he says mean things about your hair

Wyverns do it for the pay(n)

That last one made Brynn shudder. What would Phoenix do when he discovered she had run out on him? Her parents were still there under his thumb, but she did not feel as worried about that as she perhaps should. She should care about whether he took his anger out on her family, should she not? Even if she knew they would not spare a thought for her if the situation was reversed?

To harden herself against asking Mara to turn the rickshaw around, she tallied all the slights over her lifetime. Not only the snide remarks or offhand slaps, but the worse actions. Like keeping her locked up so much—if she had genuinely had no value as a bride or a daughter, why had they not let her leave? If she did not matter, why was it so important to her parents that she stayed at the family's castle?

Her younger brother, Brecon, had been a friend when they were small. But as they had grown up, he had caught on to the fact that if their parents were not belittling or punishing Brynn, they would turn their sights on him. Better to join in with the cruelty, and come up with inventive ways to torture her, than to become a target himself. Her sweet baby brother had turned into a tormenter in his own right, a smaller mirror to his parents' malice.

Everything and everyone she had come to love was used against her and turned into a weapon, until it was her own choice that she rarely left her room. So she had jumped at the lifeline when Phoenix's family started bridal negotiations, seizing a chance to see the worlds beyond her walls. An escape.

At least until Phoenix's controlling nature made itself known. Ironic, then, that it was his insistence that her family come to Spellmeet, in spite of (or because of?) their obvious contempt for humans, that allowed her to truly escape. Brynn might regret her family's treatment of her, and that the betrothal had progressed so far, but she could not regret taking a chance on Spellmeet, if it led her to freedom.

The rickshaw coming to a halt brought her out of her reverie and Brynn looked doubtfully at the shabby building before them. Not only was the roof badly repaired and missing a corner on the second level, but the smell of decay assaulted her nose. Some spell gone wrong sounded like a misbegotten choir to her aural senses. Surely Mara did not mean for her to live here?

Riley jumped out of her seat and ran to the front door, already pressing the bell repeatedly while

Brynn and Mara followed. Brynn started to question Mara but she shook her head with a secret smile before Brynn could even speak.

The door finally opened a crack and a disheveled woman peered out at them before she cried, "Oh no Mara, I've told you no more strays! Find some-where else to dump your freeloaders."

The woman tried to shut the door but Riley in-sinuated herself in the gap with a practiced move. The child grinned up at the woman who was now glaring at her, but not trying to remove her.

"This one is different, Mrs. Dibbs," Mara said. "Brynn is the answer to all your prayers."

Mrs. Dibbs mumbled, "I've heard that one be-fore," but stepped aside to let them in.

"My key to the building doesn't seem to work anymore, btw," Mara said, but only got a "hmmph" in reply.

They passed into a dim entryway and then through another door marked "Super." Mrs. Dibbs's parlor was surprisingly tidy, with doilies and deli-cate china figurines applied liberally to the prim space. A cup of tea sat cooling next to an over-stuffed chair with a book lying open over the arm. On a small table just inside the door, a cauldron bubbling with an herbal concoction did its best to cover the scent of decay.

"Well, get your spiel over with so I can get back to my book," Mrs. Dibbs grumbled. "What's so special about Brynn?"

"She can fix your troubles." Mara grinned expectantly at Mrs. Dibbs, as if she had made a dramatic pronouncement.

Mrs. Dibbs folded her arms and said, "I've heard that one before too. No one's managed yet."

"Yahbut, Brynn's a magical faerie princess," Riley said, "and she had a unicorn named Sparklewhisp who—"

"I beg your pardon, Mrs. Dibbs," Brynn interrupted before the child could deliver all her recently gained unicorn knowledge, "but has a carreg attempted to fix your 'troubles' before?"

"A what now?"

"I'll take that as a no. Would you allow me to look at your problem? It would give me a better idea whether I can fix it."

Mrs. Dibbs remained skeptical. "I don't much trust Fae these days."

"And my parents raised me to hate humans, yet here I am looking for a place to live among them." Brynn smiled sweetly as Mara chortled at her sharp retort.

The old woman sighed and waved for them all to follow her. Back through the foyer and up the stairs, where the stench and aural vibrations increased in intensity. The last few worn steps seemed to sway—or lurch—under Brynn's feet.

The nearest opening on the left was missing a door, and the view through it showed open air where an exterior wall should be. A strange blue light filled the apartment itself, cast by the glowing, throbbing ooze covering the floor. The viscous flow erupted from the side of a kitchen island and engulfed half-dissolved furniture before subsiding into the floor again, like a river seeping underground. The sound was like a laughing stream, voiced by mad sprites. Brynn frowned and walked past the doorway to see what else this place had in store.

The door on the right was closed, but a scuffling sound as they passed suggested someone might be in there. The next apartment on the left seemed to be the source of the demented choir ringing through the aural plane, and a peek through the hanging door showed a tangle of vegetation centered on a living tree with a trunk like three writhing humans. A pair of tortured eyes caught Brynn's gaze and she realized it was possible the tree *was* human in origin. Its existence grated on her with a wrongness.

No longer feeling this was an adventurous lark, Brynn turned to Mrs. Dibbs and asked, "What happened here? It does not feel like wild magic run amok."

"It's been like this since shortly after the border fell. An old woman came to the door looking for shelter and we were full up—most of my tenants had lived here for years. Good people.

"Anyway, the old woman asked me three times for hospitality and three times I refused. Then her glamour fell away and she was this beautiful—terrible—Fae lady and she cursed me and this place. It was still during the early days of the chaos and luckily her curse didn't take fully.

"One side of the building stayed the same and the other became a living hell. Any people on the cursed side got dragged into it and the others were safe—until horrors started crawling into their apartments at night. After a few disappearances and murders, the rest of my good tenants left and only the truly desperate rent here now."

"We used to live here!" Riley chirped, oblivious to how her cheerful tone clashed with the screams nearby—especially since Brynn alone could hear them.

"You are certain the changes started before the border fell?" Brynn asked.

Mrs. Dibbs shook her head. "The border had fallen before the old woman showed up. It was still in that in-between time when people hadn't noticed any uncanny travelers yet, which is why I didn't know to be on my guard for that sort of thing.

"Her curse first manifested as a darkness around the building, blocking all the light from reaching us. But we could step outside the darkness and it was fine everywhere else, so me and the tenants rallied and you'd be surprised how quickly it became our normal. Like a power outage where you could drive to the next town over and still get your Starbucks. Didn't seem like much, compared to our California wildfires and earthquakes."

Brynn frowned. "Most of the Fae would not consider a lowering darkness sufficient revenge—"

Mrs. Dibbs nodded, interrupting Brynn. "You're right. After the darkness came the other things: slugs coming out of the taps when we turned them on, the stuffing in my sofa cushions turning into writhing toads—all things designed to keep us from being comfortable in our own homes."

"That sounds more like a traditional Fae curse," Brynn said, finding that oddly comforting. "So how did it become what we see now?" She gestured to the tortured tree thing.

"Well, you know how a few days after the border fell, those pockets of wild magic started spreading, overtaking human lands? That happened around here and for a while we were an island sur-rounded by magical areas. In a weird way it was like the curse protected us, as if the wild magic flowed around a boulder.

"Then the Shifting took place—I know there are all kinds of theories about what really happened, but for all of us in the building it felt like a huge hand swept us up and rolled us like dice. When we came to a stop, the windows on one side of the building looked out on Faerie and the other onto ruins. The ruins were of Crow's Rest, a town one hundred and seventy miles from where the apart-ments had originally stood. And the curse that had taken over half the building seemed to get energy from Faerie being right outside the windows, and took on new, twisted dimensions."

"But it did not spread into any new areas of the building?"

"I told you, only one side of the building stayed cursed, but terrible things started using it as a way into the rest of the apartments. After the entire family in 2C disappeared overnight, with only pools of blood and drag marks to hint at their fate, my original tenants all moved out. I could only find sketchy tenants after that, who were less afraid of the curse than whatever else they were running from."

Had Mara been running from something worse than this cursed dwelling? Brynn glanced at her but the human avoided her gaze. Well, the answer did not affect whether Brynn could restore normalcy to Mrs. Dibb's home, so she could pursue that line of inquiry another time. For now, she would concentrate on her magic.

"I will need to go into the affected apartments," Brynn said, "in order to plan how to approach a solution."

The humans, even Riley, exchanged looks of fright and backed towards the stairs. Brynn quirked an eyebrow. "No need to worry; I do not require anyone to accompany me. But if I do not emerge after a reasonable time, it means you should all leave—if this curse is stronger than carreg magic, there is no hope for ending it."

An awkward silence filled the corridor, until the closed door they had passed opened and a hollow-eyed man stepped out. He had a bag over his shoulder and scuttled past them to the stairs. He must have heard their conversation and decided discretion was the better part of valor.

Mrs. Dibbs took Riley's hand and led her downstairs, and Mara followed with some reluctance. As for Brynn, she took a deep breath and stepped into the apartment overgrown with writhing, unnatural vegetation.

4 Avery

Nykur handed me the necklace and it felt warm in my palm. Not warm from his transferred body heat, but like his steering wheel does when he's in car form. In other words, flesh-warm.

"Are these pieces of her mountain enough to make the queen like her old self?" I asked. "Though, if we could also make her nicer that would be good too."

But Lonan and Nykur were already shaking their heads. They both looked so tired that for once I let them take a breath and gather their thoughts to answer me.

Lonan said, "I'm afraid if it does give her an energy boost, it will only be temporary. If she can help come up with a plan to end this jockeying for power in the Court, it will be worth it."

I looked again at Nykur's scar. "Was it worth it, Nykur?"

He frowned. "I owed it to Maeve to help her, as my queen and as—there was a time we were something more than ruler and subject."

"You mean..." I started to make hand gestures involving a circled finger and a rigid finger but Nykur slapped my hands down.

"It wasn't like that," he said irritably, until Lonan snickered and Nykur looked sheepish. "Okay, it was frequently like that. We were lovers, but I thought it was just a dalliance. I didn't realize how much it would hurt her when I took up with her lady in waiting, or that Tam Lin's abandonment had left her more vulnerable than I guessed."

"Was that when she sentenced you to car form at Uncle Tam's? Weird that she sent you to another former lover's."

"Maybe she thought they deserved each other," Lonan said.

Nykur shut down the side track in our conversation. "The important thing is if the queen was in her right mind now, she would do everything in her power to set things right for Faerie. Even if she knew she wasn't going to be around to see the benefits."

It was true. When I'd held her magic for a while, I'd felt the deep connection the ruler of Faerie had with the land and its creatures. Her subjects were suffering now that the magic drifted without an anchor, and it would continue like that until a legitimate ruler took the throne.

I shook my head. "If you'd told me a few years ago I'd be trying to help continue Queen Maeve's legacy, I would have scoffed hard enough to cough up a rib. But seeing how things have fallen into chaos at the Court, I might be willing to cut her some slack on some of those decisions she made in the past to keep order. Right and wrong doesn't seem as absolute as it did when I first met her."

If only I could go back in time and tell that to my younger self, too.

"Is reuniting the queen with her necklace something better done privately?" I asked. "In case she throws spells at us or something?"

Lonan gave a wry smile. "I think yelling at us is a more likely possibility, but maybe that's why it would be better to do it now. It would blend in with the rest of the yelling from the grouchy pre-lunch crowd."

The three of us made our way to Queen Maeve's room, where I wished we could at least close the door. But that would attract more attention this time of day, so we gathered around Maeve's bed and blocked the view from the hallway as much as possible.

The light filtering through the window sheers deepened the shadows under her eyes and her sunken cheekbones. Her eyes were closed and her breathing so shallow that I wondered if we'd left it too late—not that I'd even known a magical mountain necklace was an option, or I would have been out there with Nykur trying to find it.

As carefully as laying a preemie on its parent's chest for skin-to-skin contact, Lonan lined up the necklace with the queen's collarbone. We watched as it glowed briefly with a swirling light—and then it sunk into her skin, like a red velvet Oreo dropped in a glass of milk.

Maeve's eyelids snapped open, making the rest of us gasp. Her slack expression changed into a stern hardness and there was no doubt this was Queen Maeve again.

"Nephew," she asked, "how is my kingdom faring without me?"

"Not well, Your Majesty," Lonan answered.

While he and Nykur gave her a recap of what had happened since she was last lucid—when was that, like five months ago?—I watched as a healthy color returned to her flesh. Instead of classical marble, she looked like the fancy kind of stone used for kitchen countertops, with natural shading and veining. But when I took her hand, she still felt cold as a madrone tree's trunk (trust me, that's cold even in summer).

Feeling my hand on hers, she impatiently shook me off and tried to sit up. Lonan leapt to brace her with pillows, and once upright she fixed us all with a troubled (but imperious) gaze.

"We cannot allow things to continue like this in Faerie. The rightful ruler—a Sovereign—must be found and order restored."

Her tone made me fall back into my old role of smartass-in-waiting. "Yeah, we figured out that much. So point us to them and we'll start a campaign fund drive."

Her gaze narrowed, but she fell back into her diplomatic way of addressing my meaning (and not my mockery). "I am afraid it is not as simple as me naming a successor; the magic of the Fae ruler will only settle on a worthy soul. Although someone can physically occupy the throne and oversee the Court, they are not a true, united ruler without the

Sovereignty anchored by them. The next ruler will have to be quite different from those in the past and will have to co-exist with humans in an entirely new way, now that Merlin's machinations have left our lands commingled. They will need to have an understanding of both worlds."

Lonan and I exchanged a glance, and his cry of, "But Auntie Maeve, I can't—" overlapped my, "Not it!" before the queen frowned us into silence again.

"You would better serve the Court by searching for the true candidate. I do not believe either of you have the traits necessary to rule Faerie."

Wait, did she just call us losers? Lonan is royal too, for fu— Nykur's elbow in my ribs dissipated the indignation building in me. He'd learned that trick when my wild magic was building, back in the days when I still had it but didn't have any control. Okay, so self-control was still an issue for me.

I rubbed my side and asked, "How do you know, Your Majesty?"

"Although I have lost my magic and the mantle of ruler, I can still feel...the web of connections, like a phantom limb. Whoever the Sovereign is, they are not nearby, but they do exist."

Nykur said, "You can help us find them, then."

Her gaze softened and she reached to stroke his dark hair. "I am afraid not. I am burning through this remnant of my mountain as we speak and I do not have long."

So, what, do we trick the Court into coming to view her body, and see if her corpse makes a sound like a metal detector when the right one comes near?

Before I could ask anything as disrespectful as that, I remembered some advice from the counselor my mom had made me go to. "Before you speak, ask yourself, 'is it true, is it helpful, is it kind?'" In my case, she had also added, "Are you making a joke to deflect from the intensity of your own emotions?"

While I wrestled myself for a little bit of truthfulness/helpfulness/kindness, Lonan and Nykur had been asking more pertinent questions about how to recognize a Sovereign. But I could see even in that short time, the Queen was losing substance. Her cheekbones weren't nearly as sharp, and when she reached up to sweep a lock of hair from her face, both the lock of hair and the fingertip crumbled away.

I wasn't sure if she noticed, but Nykur did. He came to stand beside me and whispered, "It was foolish of me, but I hoped the necklace would do more to help her. To be honest, I hoped it would strengthen her enough to take over Faerie again."

I wrapped my arms around one of his and laid my head against his bicep (he was too tall for me to put it on his shoulder). The way Lonan was holding himself, I knew he had noticed his aunt's failing strength too. Nykur and I let them have their time together, and I was surprised at the tears starting in my eyes. Even while I was watching it happen, I couldn't believe someone like Queen Maeve could just...stop being.

Nykur patted my hand and I whispered, "However much she chapped my ass, she doesn't deserve to go like this. Maybe it should have been in battle, or an orgy gone wrong or something, but not this sad fading."

Nykur whispered back, "It's actually called 'dwindling' among the oread. It's not painful, as far as I know. Just a gradual loss of memories and self."

Like that isn't awful enough?? I shuddered.

"Your Majesty," I said as I approached the bed again. She turned a dazzling smile on me and then *poof!* there was only some sparkling sand settling on her pillow. The Queen was gone and Lonan's hand, which had been resting on her crossed arms, thumped onto the blankets.

At the swirling dust motes, I fell to my knees. *That's it? No fanfare when a queen dies?* Only Lonan to hang his head while Nykur came over to gently smooth the blankets, and then the sound of me screaming out my anger, grief, frustration, and guilt. But somehow getting it out didn't mean there was any less of it still inside, waiting.

Mrs. Shore came to see what happened, and fortunately she knew and trusted her employees, like me (aka Cally) and Lonan (Starling), enough to believe our explanation of Maeve's final moments. Or maybe that was due to seeing enough weirdness when the border fell, so our story didn't seem so out there after all. In any case, she gave us the rest of the afternoon off to grieve since she knew we'd had a special relationship with Maeve.

We left Mrs. Shore with Nykur, who was willing to help clean up *(with what, the hand vac?)* and Lonan led my shaking form to the kitchen to make me a cup of tea.

"Wait," I said, "she was your aunt—shouldn't I be making you a cup of tea?"

"I want something to do with my hands," he said, and for once there was no accompanying suggestive lift of his eyebrow.

So he brought my tea and came and sat at the stainless-steel prep counter with me. The rest of the staff had already taken the lunches into the dining room, and sat down to eat with the residents, so it was quiet here as we each stared into our cooling mugs.

"We have to do something," I blurted finally. And there was the raised eyebrow, this time to show Lonan was skeptical.

"That's it?" He asked. "You're done grieving and ready to move on now?"

So many feelings and words tried to come out my mouth at once that they stumbled over each other. "No! It's because I want to honor Queen Maeve that I—I'm ready to try to make a difference again, instead of hiding here and feeling sorry for myself. I want to—no, I need to—help find the next ruler of Faerie, like she said."

Thankfully, Lonan was used to parsing my outbursts. "Okay. How do you propose we do that?"

I rotated my mug with one hand and didn't look at him. "Well, I don't have a plan yet. But...Aunt Queenie said something about the true monarch needing to be familiar with the human world and Faerie. Doesn't it sound like Spellmeet would be the perfect training ground for someone like that? I mean, from what Missa tells me, that place is forcing all kinds of adaptations. It would be worth checking out, right? And we were working here mostly for Maeve's sake anyway."

"So you'd abandon Mrs. Shore and everyone else? They need help."

It was true—we couldn't turn our backs on our created family. It had been hard enough to leave my mom behind, and I wasn't sure if I could pull it off again.

"Maybe we could find someone to fill in for us?" I sounded unconvincing even to my own ears. "The circus here would feel like a calm oasis to Nykur, after his time at Court."

Which is pretty much how Nykur put it, when we went to go ask him. We found him taking a dip in the garden pond—with every resident's face pressed to the windows to get a good luck at his muscular form.

"I'll cover for you," he said as he dried off, "as long as your plan has a good chance of working. What is your plan?"

They both looked at me expectantly. "Um, to go to Spellmeet and find the next ruler?"

The silenced lengthened until Nykur figured out that was all I had. "Do you have a death wish, Avery? Going to Spellmeet is risky enough, what with everyone after you—but to go in with no real idea of what comes next? Lonan, how are you okay with this—"

"Hey, she's her own human—"

"She's her own human who is standing right here and can answer for herself," I interrupted. "Truth is, I don't think this is something we can plan too closely. Queen Maeve said the new ruler will need to be different, and if we go in with a plan there's a good chance we'll only be looking for what we expect. But maybe we need to have some faith that Faerie's magic is trying already, and our part is to help make a connection."

Lonan shook his head. "Okay, now I hear the crazy talk. We can't really go in there thinking that we can, what, set up a ruler-finding app? Thronematch.com or something?"

I sighed and dropped onto a bench on the pond's shore. "I'm not saying we shouldn't have any kind of plan at all. I'm saying we can't make a plan from here—we only have second- or third-hand accounts of what Spellmeet is like right now. What if the wild magic or queen's magic causing all the trouble there could recognize me? And what if I can help, like, point it to the next ruler?"

"That's a lot of ifs," Nykur said. "And you've left out the biggest hurdle: how do you and Lonan walk around Spellmeet when everyone will grab their torches and pitchforks at the sight of you?"

"Duh, Lonan uses a glamour on both of us—"

They both shook their heads and Lonan said, "It won't stand up. The magic is too chaotic there, and a lot of humans with the Sight gravitate to Spellmeet. We'd be caught out for sure."

I glowered at them like they were busing in Sighted humans to thwart me. "Fine, then I'll need your help, but it isn't only me who owes Queen Maeve. We all want to fix this, right?"

They made sounds of agreement and I continued, "So get the polyjuice potion brewing or whatever, because I'm going to Spellmeet."

"That's not a real spell." Nykur waved his hand dismissively. "Not that it worked faultlessly in the books either."

Lonan ignored the aside. "Avery, you haven't been to Spellmeet. Do you remember when the wild magic pockets were expanding, gobbling up Crow's Rest and other places? The human military and Fae soldiers tried to stop it, and after the Shifting they didn't understand why it had stopped.

"To make sure an incursion like that didn't catch anyone unawares again, the two armies set up a hard border around Spellmeet, with checkpoints and zones. They would love to keep a close headcount of anyone inside the barriers, so they know when someone disappears or if they ever need to evacuate everyone, but there are too many ways into Faerie now to keep track.

"But we can't use those back doors because even a hint of your presence in Faerie would set off alarms and traps. Glamour won't fool them, and neither will spells—the best minds have turned their attention to catching Avery Flynn, Most Wanted."

I sighed. "Okay, so Faerie is out. But there has to be a way for us to move around Spellmeet safely. This should be easy for you, Lonan, since you're always bragging about your past as a spy and a strategist. What would your crafty corbin-self do?"

Lonan's eyes unfocused as he thought it through. "I could always make us masks. They should hold up in Spellmeet."

Nykur asked, "You mean..." and Lonan nodded.

Nykur laughed as their gazes met. "She'll never go along with it. She'll hate it."

"Go along with what?" I asked, Nykur's glee making me suspicious.

Lonan smiled and said, "Leave it to me."

I didn't like how wicked-Fae his smile made him look. That couldn't be good, right?

5 Brynn

Brynn sifted through the cacophony in the room, the sounds of magic gone wrong. The overgrown plants traced back to the human world, probably harmless vines and sprouts without the influence of the Fae magic running amok here. Truly, they wanted to grow naturally again, without the magic forcing them into their role of tormentors.

Brynn easily tuned in to what must have been the original curse, as it showed the touch of a single, malevolent Fae. Clawed fingers plucking on a harp string, the evil intent thrumming with an undiminishing vibration. It would continue until the end of time, or until its maker stilled it—unless a carreg like Brynn stepped in and set things aright.

Although she readily identified the curse and its effects, untangling the strings took some time. As she worked, Brynn's fingers stroked the air, gently coaxing the sounds into order. What had been a symphony where each player struck a different chord, a symphony where keys and scales had no conductor, became instead a more harmonious composition.

But something was keeping Brynn from fixing it entirely; some other magic disrupted her efforts to tune. Like blares of a trumpet solo intruding from another apartment, some other magic sounded in the space.

Frowning in concentration, Brynn followed the sly chords and ran her fingers along them for but an instant—but it was long enough to recognize the sinuous melody of wild magic. She knew from experience she would not be able to quiet it; all she could do was try to isolate it from her other work.

The wild magic allegroed away, staying just out of her reach; as long as it did not interfere with her task, that was fine. She had worked for a few more verses when a new beat drumrolled into frame. Brynn sighed as it sowed chaos in her carefully ordered composition, but then she paused.

This was wild magic also, but with a completely different signature than the earlier occurrence.

How was that even possible? Where had this other player come from, when everyone knew it was Avery Flynn's wild magic alone which had caused so much irreversible destruction? This new strain was more strident than the other wild magic—a bassoon of gravitas compared to the sprightly tin whistle and rambunctiousness of the first one—and the duo were definitely not working in concert.

Her hard work started to decrescendo as she hesitated, unused to working around two strong wild magics. Was she up to the challenge? Her mother's voice, on a loop in her head, assured her she was not. *That she was worthless and useless and a disgrace*—Brynn took a shaky breath and tried to get ahold of herself.

Apparently, escaping her mother's influence was not going to be accomplished merely by leaving her behind. Lady Massif may not even have realized her daughter was gone, and yet her poison still affected Brynn. It had the power to disrupt her life as surely as the wild magic was disrupting her spellwork.

But in both cases, Brynn only lost if she stopped trying. After all, with her sheltered—isolated—upbringing, many things would likely be unfamiliar or unsettling. She would have to adjust, or her family would be proved right about her. As Mara had said, didn't Brynn want to find out how brave she could be without her family bullying her? She could only discover that by doing her best at whatever task she set herself to, no matter how unfamiliar or unsettling it was.

Brynn consciously tuned out the chorus of criticism—she would not let her mother's words shape who she would be now. With a deep breath, she squared her shoulders and picked up the strings again, restoring some harmony to the magic in her grasp. The wild magics (one like a mischievous ferret and one like a blundering bull) still gallivanted around her work, but the non-wild magics she had gathered gained strength, forming a crowded stave of notes like a picket fence to keep the wild magics out.

But still they broke through again and again, testing Brynn's patience. Finally the "wilder" of the wild magics got distracted and romped off to some other roguery, leaving her only one to deal with. Things went much faster after that and Brynn breathed a sigh of relief, like air escaping a piper's bag. She had never worked so long or hard on righting a curse before that she had actually broken into a sweat.

In one final measure, her magic and the original state of the apartment aligned, and the harpstring of the curse stilled. The overgrown plants rustled with the fading vibrations, and then retreated from the room, letting in the warm light of the rising sun. The sunlight struck the trunk of the tree and consumed it in a flurry of sparkling dust, which left three humans huddled together on the floor.

The smallest one began to cry.

Footsteps pounded up the stairs and Mara cautiously peered into the apartment's doorway. Her wide eyes darted around the more-normal dwelling, until she noticed the humans comforting each other.

"Is it over?" she asked.

"It should be," Brynn answered. "I can go check the other apartments."

Mara moved aside so Brynn could exit, and Brynn added, "Those people need you and it is safe for you to go in."

Mara stepped inside as Brynn continued to the other apartments; the glowing blue ooze in the first one was gone. The furniture and fixtures were still eaten away where it had flowed, but her magic did not fix that kind of thing. Another Fae would have to come in to restore them, or the humans would have to physically remove the damaged items.

The other apartments looked innocent now as well—if you ignored the bloodstains or other signs of the curse. Brynn caught herself smiling, proud that she had managed to defeat the strong magic and restore order, as her carreg kind were meant to do. Like she had never been allowed or encouraged to do, until she escaped to Spellmeet.

Shuffling sounds in the hallway made Brynn turn back to see Mara supporting the humans from the tree trunk as they moved towards the staircase. The family did not seem to want to let go of each other, so Mara urged them along as one unit.

Brynn stepped over to help, but the family showed the whites of their eyes and keened softly.

"I think it's best if they don't have any contact with Fae right away," Mara said apologetically. "I'll take them to the Silver Cross shelter, where they can get the right kind of help. Mrs. Dibbs said for you to come see her, please."

Brynn waited until the family made it out the front door before she descended the stairs and found Mrs. Dibbs's Super apartment again.

Mrs. Dibbs answered the door with a wide smile, welcoming Brynn inside.

"Can I make you some tea? Are you hungry, dear?"

Brynn could not help noticing the contrast between the grudging welcome from before, but she was indeed hungry.

"Yes, please, some refreshment would be welcome," Brynn answered, her tiredness making her revert to more formal speech. "And Mara said you wanted to speak to me?"

Mrs. Dibbs flapped her hands in Brynn's direction, herding her to a chair. "Let me get our tray first. Then we can talk business."

Brynn seated herself on a doilied ottoman, but stood again as she spied the shelves of books lining the walls. A few human titles had occasionally made their way to her family's castle, but Lady Massif destroyed many of them before Brynn even had a chance to see what their pages held. The few she had managed to hoard were currently at the bottom of her trunk, left behind.

Brynn's well-worn copies of romance novels and a book on the secret lives of bats (missing several pages, unfortunately) were nothing to Mrs. Dibbs's library. Brynn pulled out several at random and discovered that many of them had their genre helpfully labeled on the back covers.

Romance novels dominated this collection as well, but Brynn had no idea there were so many sub-types. And mystery novels, and science-based fiction, and even some stories meant for readers much younger than Mrs. Dibbs's advanced years. Plus, books on nature (a complete copy of the bat book!) and biographies of notable humans in history. Even some poetry and "mythology," which could rightly be called biographies of notable Fae in history.

The sound of Mrs. Dibbs returning made Brynn hurry to reshelve the book in her hand. Her hostess set a tray on a small table between straight-backed chairs, so Brynn took a seat in one of those. The steam from the teacup tickled Brynn's nostrils enticingly, although the sandwiches had an odd smell.

"I hope you like tuna salad," Mrs. Dibbs said as she put a half-sandwich on a plate for Brynn, and then continued to chatter about nonsensical things.

Brynn listened with half an ear while she surreptitiously peeked between the bread. Shreds of some kind of meat swam in a white, gooey bath, dotted with green tidbits. She had not had much opportunity to try human food, but this bore no resemblance to the fancy dinner from the restaurant Phoenix had invited her family to. That meal had been more...distinct, not so commingled as this offering.

Deciding it would be rude to refuse, Brynn took a bite—and immediately regretted it. The shreds were briny and flavorful, as were the green bits in a different way, but the white substance was oily and rancid. She drew on all her years of not reacting to her mother's slights in order to not show her revulsion.

The lubricated bite slid down her throat, and Brynn was relieved when Mrs. Dibbs addressed her and gave her an excuse to set the sandwich back down.

"I never thought I would see this building as a real home again," Mrs. Dibbs was saying. "I know the Fae don't like to have outstanding debts, so what can I do to repay you? Within reason, of course, and I get to agree or disagree."

Brynn had to smile; Mrs. Dibbs had obviously had some dealings with Fae in the past. And Brynn's work certainly had value in Spellmeet, according to Mara, so what would be a fair trade? She had no idea whether to ask for another cup of tea or Mrs. Dibbs's soul.

"Would access to your books be a fair trade?" Brynn asked. "I should like to read more human stories."

Mrs. Dibbs was visibly relieved by the proposal. "Yes, I think that would reasonable. I was going to offer you a discount on rent, but lending you my books is better. You do still want to live here, don't you?"

"At least for a time, until I get more familiar with Spellmeet. Which apartments are vacant?"

Mrs. Dibbs led her out of the Super apartment and showed her a few spaces on the ground floor, and when none of those suited Brynn they moved up to the second floor. Brynn ended up choosing an apartment with mysterious blood smears, as the majority of the furniture was intact and it was unlikely the original occupants would be back for it.

Mrs. Dibbs rummaged under the kitchen sink and found some cleaning supplies for Brynn to use, and was instructing her in their use when Mara appeared in the doorway.

She set the bag she was carrying on the countertop and asked, "So this is your apartment now?"

Brynn smiled and nodded. "Yes! And Mrs. Dibbs has agreed lending me her books is a fair trade for my services."

Mara narrowed her eyes. "Is that so? And what about rent?"

Mrs. Dibbs did not answer, just glared at Mara with her arms crossed, so Brynn answered, "The books are in lieu of a discount on rent, I believe?"

Brynn looked back and forth between Mara and Mrs. Dibbs as they seemed to wage some sort of battle with their gazes.

Mara broke into a sly grin and said, "Or I can teach you how public libraries work, Brynn, and then I'll take the free rent as my finder's fee. I can have entire families moved in here by this after-noon."

"Now wait a minute!" Mrs. Dibbs sputtered. "A finder's fee is not worth the same as what Brynn did."

"It's not?" Mara's brow furrowed in consternation.

"Of course not! Brynn made this place habitable again, when no one else could, and all you did was point her in my direction. I'll be able to move paying tenants in again, once these places are cleaned up. If anyone is entitled to free rent, it's not you, it's Brynn."

Now Mara stepped close to Brynn and whispered, "Say you accept the free rent. She's cheating you with only the books. You can still get books at the library."

Mrs. Dibbs said, "Wait—"

But Brynn hurriedly interrupted her and said, "Your counteroffer of free rent is accepted."

Mrs. Dibbs grumbled at Mara before stomping out the door. Mara let out a wicked chuckle and danced a triumphant little jig.

Brynn smiled in spite of her worry about a vengeful Mrs. Dibbs, but Mara said, "Don't worry, she's actually an old softie. That's how I put some of my strays here over the last months, in spite of how cheap Mrs. Dibbs is."

"Your strays?" Brynn asked.

"Yeah," Mara said as she started digging in the bag she had brought. "I seem to have a knack for finding people and creatures who need help—or they find me. And then I connect them to something they need. It's like a whole business for me now."

"Well, I am certainly grateful for your help. Do I owe you anything, a finder's fee?"

"I'll bring my toaster by later and you can fix that, please. Now, are you hungry?"

Mara showed Brynn the items she had pulled out of the bag. "I got you a few shelf-stable things to tide you over until you know more what you like to eat here. And I suspect it would be better to throw that refrigerator out without opening it."

Brynn recognized the loaf of bread wrapped in plastic, but was wary of the jars marked "peanut butter" and "jelly."

"Mrs. Dibbs offered me a tuna salad sandwich earlier but it was not to my liking. Are those things similar?"

Mara shuddered. "Mrs. Dibbs's tuna salad is in a class by itself—or maybe its own phylum? I think you'll like this better. I prefer strawberry jam but Riley insisted I bring you her favorite, grape jelly.

"Here, take a sniff and see what you think."

The seals released audibly and Brynn hesitantly moved her face closer to the jars. Both smelled delicious, so she smiled in approval.

"Now, do you know how to make a PB&J sandwich?"

Mara's question was without judgement, so Brynn did not feel too foolish about shaking her head. And after her new friend showed her how to spread the thick nut butter and sticky jelly, a delicious combination rewarded Brynn's tastebuds.

"Much better," she said rudely through a mouthful.

Mara clapped her hands and then pitched in on cleaning up Brynn's new apartment.

6 Brynn

Even a chore like cleaning was more fun with Mara involved. She had found a pair of dust-covered speakers and plugged her phone in. Music was the best way to refresh and calm a carreg, and perhaps Mara had sensed this. Or maybe Mara wanted the music for herself and it was a fortunate coincidence?

Either way, they made swift progress, tackling the bloodstains first. Then all the previous owners' personal possessions and photographs got boxed up, along with the decorations not to Brynn's taste. Mara was going to take them to Mrs. Dibbs, so they could be used in a future memorial service for the couple who had lived there. Mara had not known them very well, as they had moved in after she and

Riley had moved out, but felt that no one should pass without it being marked in some way.

It was strange learning about the humans only from their possessions. The woman was near Brynn's size for clothing and she would have been tempted to keep some things herself, but the raiment tended to lots of sparkles and sequins. Brynn was not against a bit of flash, if it enhanced the look, but these seemed like perfectly serviceable shirts that a jeweled creature had exploded upon.

And every one of the man's shirts had food stains down the front. Mara tried to make a contest of guessing the source of the stain, but since Brynn was not familiar with most human food it was fairly one-sided. Mara and Brynn also kept finding empty or half-full bottles of alcohol stashed in odd places, so they learned at least one of the former tenants liked a secret tipple.

When Brynn asked Mara the purpose of the objects found in one of the bedside tables, Mara giggled uncontrollably as she explained. But Brynn shocked her when she winked and put them back.

"You might want to run those through the dishwasher and put in new batteries, if you're serious about keeping them," Mara warned. "Or buy new ones."

Brynn's only answer was a cryptic smile; even a sheltered Fae's upbringing did not include prudish human mores about lovers and sex toys. Her marriage with Phoenix would have allowed for other partners—unless her wyvern fiancé had taken on the human idea of monogamy. Doubtful that would be the human value to stick, since it was so contrary to Fae ways.

It took both Mara and Brynn to wrestle the refrigerator to the top of the stairs, where they left it until Mara could recruit some friends with an appliance dolly. Mrs. Dibbs emerged from her Super apartment with a stack of doilies for Brynn, and told her she could still access the books whenever she wanted, so the landlady must not have been too put out by the changed terms of their arrangement. In a fit of reciprocal goodwill, Brynn said she only expected the free rent for a few months, while she set up her livelihood.

By the time the apartment was sparkling clean, if a little sparse-looking, it was late afternoon and Mara had to go change for work at the restaurant. Her absence left the apartment quiet and bereft, and Brynn was suddenly exhausted—physically and emotionally. She had been able to keep her worries at bay with the constant activity since her escape the night before, but now they came back full force.

Would Phoenix connect Brynn's disappearance with Mara and Riley, thereby making them a target of revenge also? Or would Brynn's family take the full brunt of his bride's humiliating departure? Brynn's instincts told her Phoenix would rather keep the incident quiet, and her family would most definitely wash their hands of her.

Sadly, Brynn had received far more kindness from the handful of humans she had dealt with over the last day, than she had ever felt from her family over her lifetime. Even bristly Mrs. Dibbs was not as hard as she tried to seem.

As a child, it was the nursemaids, the humans stolen away to Faerie to serve the powerful families, who had shown Brynn any tenderness. Most of them had been women torn from their kin and they may have attached to Brynn because they missed their own babes, but they did not have to be kind. In fact, they were often punished for fostering "weakness" in the Fae children. None of the humans, kind or otherwise, stayed long enough to make a real difference in Brynn's life.

Brynn sighed and scrubbed her tears away. She rifled through the drawers of clothes she had kept and picked something silky to sleep in, crawling between the clean sheets she and Mara had put on the bed. Dust still prickled at her nostrils, but around

her the sounds of the building were a soft lullaby of harmonious magic.

Noises from the kitchen woke Brynn the next morning. She sleepily snuggled under the covers, until she remembered she now lived alone. The thought that the previous occupants may have come back after all made her bolt out of bed, ready to defend her space. Oreads were highly territorial, even away from their mountains.

Brynn picked up a lamp and tiptoed over to the door, peering out. Drawers opened and closed, and the long *scraaaape* of a chair being dragged over a hard floor sounded. Riley's untidy head appeared above the counter and Brynn relaxed her grip on her makeshift weapon.

Setting it down, she went to join her visitor. "What are you doing here so early, little one?"

Riley continued her careful spreading of peanut butter on a slice of bread. "It's not early, it's ten o'clock! Mara told me to help you make some sammiches for work today. She stopped by Mrs. Dibbs's but she'll be here in a minute."

The child added a sandwich to the pile on the counter, and Brynn took one. It tasted as good as she remembered and she could not help making a little moan of pleasure.

"Grape jelly is the best, right?" Riley asked, licking the purple goo off the knife before dipping it back into the jar.

Brynn nodded, her mouth full, but wanting to ask what work Mara had in mind for today. Before she could swallow, Mara herself was there and launched into an itinerary.

"First up is my place and you curing that damned singing toaster. Then after I eat some toast with butter and silence, we can write up some simple business cards for you and go around to hand them out. You might need to do a few freebie carreg things until word gets out about you, is that okay?"

Brynn smiled wryly. "Considering they have never been valued in the past, that is fine. When do we leave?"

Mara looked full-on at Brynn's silky nightgown and color rose in her cheeks. "You'll need to change or people won't be able to concentrate long enough to hear your pitch. Wear something dark, something serious-looking?"

Mara's voice got a little huskier at the end of the sentence, and Brynn's own cheeks warmed, conflicted. She was open to a liaison with Mara, but what were proper courtship rites for humans? In Faerie, there were not "proper" rites between Fae and humans because the Fae had all the power in the relationships. The power to take what they wanted, or to glamour the weaker humans into believing what they wanted them to. Being so soft-hearted, Brynn had never been comfortable with that arrangement, so she had never been with a human.

Brynn added a little extra swish to her hips as she walked away, in case Mara liked that, and went to change. The left-behind clothing did not look serious enough with all the sparkles, even though she had saved only the most unadorned of the lot. So Brynn put her dark corset and skirt back on, adding a simple gold chain as a belt. Plus a choker and wrist bangles from the jewelry box which came with the apartment.

As she leaned over the vanity to check her reflection in the mirror, the discarded wig caught her eye. Placing it on top of her own dark hair, she attempted to arrange it into a style. But it only laid there like a hairy trophy draped over her head. Obviously she was not doing it right, but Mara should know how to fix it.

When she emerged, Riley laughed out loud at the wig slipping off Brynn's head, parading with a paper towel draped over her own hair. Mara showed a little more restraint and stifled a smile as she said, "Um, that's not how to wear it."

Brynn raised one eyebrow and said, "Really?" trying to match Mara's tone when she was at her most sarcastic.

Mara shook her head and said, "Okay, we can add a stop at the hairdresser's today and she can color your hair into something like that. If it's what you want."

"I like the purple," Riley said before Brynn could answer. "It makes her eyes look less like they're undead."

"My eyes look dead?"

Mara winced. "No, Riley reads zombie comic books so she means your eyes look like—but yours aren't creepy like that—your irises are just a really light silver. The purple does add some contrast, though."

Although she had tried to make up for the child's honesty, Mara's stumbling words—not precisely a compliment—only left Brynn feeling more self-conscious. Perhaps she had been misreading Mara's signals and all the blushing was from discomfort rather than attraction? Disgust caused by her obviously non-human eyes? Or, she could have misjudged Mara entirely and she was not one of the good humans.

Brynn had begun to think she could possibly fit in here, only to discover a feature she could not change was off-putting. Subdued now, Brynn said, "I will get a jacket and we can go."

As she picked one out, she could hear a whispered conversation in the kitchen—well, Mara whispered and Riley said things like "What did I do?" in a shouted whisper—and the child greeted her with an apology for hurting her feelings.

"It is fine," Brynn said tightly. "I think I am nervous about going out, and perhaps a little more sensitive because of it. We should go."

Mara and Riley did not say much as they rode in the rickshaw to their home. Brynn tried to pretend the tears still filling her eyes were from the wind of their travel, and not because a few words from a human child had reduced her to the forlorn Fae child she used to be.

As they turned onto a street, Brynn could have picked out Mara's house without prompting. It stood out among the plainer homes in the neighborhood, with its wooden trim painted in fanciful colors. But Brynn would have guessed it was Mara's by its air of refuge and charm, and its welcoming aural song restored her.

As they passed through the sizable front yard, Brynn's eye recognized Fae plants as well as human ones. Glowbells, a favorite napping place for pixies, nuzzled up to ragged daisies dotted with ladybugs.

An iridescent cobravine intertwined with a wild rose, the only human plant persistent enough to withstand it. But the stand of dark-winged maples along the fence gave her pause; even though it was a Fae plant, it only affected humans—by putting them into a deep, dreamless sleep they may never awaken from.

"Mara, do you know that plant? It is very dangerous."

Mara barely glanced at it as she continued to the front steps. "I don't do much with the plants, that's Aurora's job. But everything she grows has a use, so I trust she knows what she's doing."

Brynn looked closer as she passed through the rest of the garden, and noticed faces watching her: the sly glances of flower fairies among the blossoms, plus the inquisitive nose of a hedgehog beneath a hydrangea-leaf umbrella. The cats were hardest to spot, with only their unblinking eyes peering from the shadows—and there were a lot of cats. Mostly black ones.

As Brynn crossed the porch, something stirred in a house tucked under the eaves, and a wizened brownie stared curiously down at her. She smiled back; if a brownie had taken up residence here, it was a blessed household indeed. They only gave up their wandering for places and people who had tru-ly earned their trust.

Once inside, Riley tried to drag Brynn off to show her her bedroom, but Mara firmly said, "Toaster first. You can show her all your stuffed unicorns while I eat my toast."

Stuffed unicorns? Did the child really have pre-served unicorn bodies in her bedroom? That seemed like an extreme obsession if that was the case. But Brynn put it out of her mind as Mara led her into the kitchen, redolent with the smells of Fae and human cooking. Were those rubyplum tarts she smelled? She had not had one of those since she was a child.

But the song of the toaster soon held her com-plete attention. An annoying tinny voice rang out, in spite of the layers of towels attempting to muffle it. Clashing with the voice was the underlying mag-ic, a spell crafted expressly to annoy but not harm.

"What did you do to deserve this spell?" Brynn asked, amused such a small magic could so success-fully get under Mara's skin.

"I offended a pooka by singing in the shower; apparently he's not a fan of the Bunny Foo-foo song. It's about some rogue pooka getting royally punished and isn't meant to be sung casually I guess? Anyways, he thought making my toaster sing dirges at me was an appropriate punishment."

Brynn stifled a laugh; that was definitely a typical pooka joke. "And you were not able to find him again to apologize and ask him to remove the spell?"

"Oh no, the bastard still lives here. And I've apologized but he thinks it's too funny to keep torturing me."

"As long as he does not turn his disappointment on me, I will fix it." Brynn concentrated and stilled the discordant notes of the spell.

Mara's eyes widened, as if she did not dare believe it could be that simple to have a normal toaster again. She unwrapped it and held up the chrome appliance reverently. Other residents poked their heads around the door frame, drawn by the absence of singing.

A clatter of hooves sounded on the stairs and a pooka burst in the room, saying, "Hey, who undid my spell—" but came to a halt when he spied Brynn.

They stared at each other and Brynn braced herself for some retaliation, but he shrugged and said, "A carreg. Fair enough, if you went to the trouble to track one down."

Mara said, "Truce?"

The pooka grinned slyly and clopped up the stairs, and the other residents went back to what they were doing too. Did anyone else notice the pooka had not actually agreed to the truce?

"Exactly how many people live here?" Brynn asked as she watched Mara load bread slices into the toaster.

Mara shrugged. "It varies on any given day. Me and Riley, plus maybe six permanent residents in the house, and as many in the gardens. Most of the Fae and humans wash up here when they're in need, and they only stay until they don't need the help anymore. Kind of a waystation for misfits."

"Misfits like me? So why am I staying at Mrs. Dibbs's then?"

Mara winked as she pulled her slightly burnt toast out of the slots. "Because Mrs. Dibbs needed you to clear her building more than we needed another mouth to feed. Plus, you said you didn't leave your home castle much, so I thought you'd like your own space."

Before Brynn could voice what she herself needed, Riley dragged her off to her room. Fortunately the stuffed unicorns were only toys, but unfortunately it took a quarter hour for Riley to name each and every one for Brynn.

Halfway through, she heard the pooka chuckling from the room next door, like he thought that was punishment enough for ruining his toaster gag.

7 Avery

It was going to take Lonan a few days to get things together for the masks he was making us, so I used the time to show Nykur all the duties he'd be responsible for. But it quickly became obvious he had strict boundaries on what he was willing to do, and money (not that there was a lot to go around) wasn't a real incentive to a Fae. He was a decent Fae in a lot of ways, but face it: working at a care home meant that on some days you'd be up to your elbows in nasty shit, and that wasn't a euphemism. Enough said.

The plan to have Nykur cover all our duties obviously wasn't going to work. Mrs. Shore grumbled, but ended up giving the hours to more-willing employees and we let Nykur take on the jobs which needed muscle or magic. He was good at both of those. Lonan's and my absence would still be felt, but what else could we do? Stopping the Fae Civil War was really important—though we didn't tell Mrs. Shore that's what we were doing.

She thought we just needed a vacation, since it's easy to get burnt out in this line of work. And time to process our grief—and all the other emotions—from Maeve's death. Good for Mrs. Shore for supporting us in that.

It would be a lie to say I wasn't looking forward to a break. In my time at Shady Grove, I'd discovered hard, constant work was a great way to calm my fidgeting, like meditation for my twitchy muscles. Helping others also got me out of my own head, which even without the wild magic's influence was not always a pleasant place to spend much time. Especially when my snark turned inward, so much harder on myself than I was on other people.

I'd been feeling extra restless lately; staying here to take care of Maeve had begun to weigh on me like a prison sentence. Okay, one I'd earned, but along with the grief over her death came a huge feeling of relief over not seeing her fade anymore. The smaller losses were a reminder of the big things she—we—had lost. Maybe that's why I was so eager to find the next ruler—if we succeeded, I might finally be able to look ahead to some kind of happily ever after.

Fortunately, since he didn't have as many duties after all, Nykur decided to torture me with vague-but-ominous comments about the masks Lonan was making. Sometimes he'd snigger in a really annoying way if I walked into the room while Lonan and Nykur were talking to each other. Then there was the time when we were eating dinner and he did his best to stifle his laughter, but ended up only making Mrs. Shore think he was choking. Her Heimlich maneuver only brought up a belly laugh and now she trusted him even less.

And Lonan didn't help lay my worries to rest, since he seemed to be regressing to some darker version of himself while he worked on this spell. His eyes were the furthest from human that I'd ever seen them—well, not his eyes, but the sentience behind them. If you looked too long, you got lost in overgrown forest paths, running from the crows hidden in the shadowed branches.

If he'd been like this when I first met him, no way would I have fallen in love with him. I made the mistake of saying that to Nykur and he sighed and said, "Look, you told me yourself you're feeling stifled and stuck here, especially about not being able to show your true self, since everyone wants your true self to die.

"Well, Lonan has been doing that since he met you. He came here weaker when the spell with Daniel went wrong, and we all know you like a bad boy—but what about a monster? What about the Lonan who was the Butcher Bird and feared by humans and Fae? He's had to shove that side of him deep down, because otherwise he's afraid he'll lose you. You're basically getting the weaker version of him all the time, even though he has his full powers to draw on.

"This spell he's working on is pretty dark, and he's modifying it to make it more, um, palatable to you." He interrupted his serious talk to let out a chuckle, and then got ahold of himself. "He cares about you too much to lose himself to darkness, but if you don't learn to at least tolerate Darth Lonan both of you may come to regret it."

I heard what he was saying and would spend some time working on it; after all, I had eventually come to terms with my own dark wyvern side. But Nykur's words did not make me any less nervous to see these masks when Lonan finished them. The buildup had me missing sleep and even a few meals, which was unheard of for me. But finally, Lonan told me to meet him in the kitchen around midnight, and I dragged myself there.

I had no idea what to expect—had he really made a pair of masks, or did he track down some ancient, evil-possessed death masks? Were they like enchanted red shoes and we'd never be able to get them off without chopping off our heads? Because who knew if a corbin could survive that, but no way I could without my wild magic. I still trusted Lonan, but I wasn't sure if I trusted whatever magic he was using.

Under the fluorescent lights in the kitchen, Lonan looked like he was back to his normal self, or at least a tired version of his normal self. He smiled at me and I smiled back reflexively, but it faded when I saw the two roasting pans in front of him, covered with kitchen towels.

"You look kinda green; are you sure about this?" he asked. "I don't mind the wasted time if you want to back out."

"No, I—I just don't know what to expect," I said. "Nykur's been hinting you're using black magic or something and maybe I don't want this after all?"

Lonan shook his head. "He's messing with you—mostly. The original spell was pretty dark—definitely nasty—but I've made some substitutions.

You still may not like it, but at least it won't damage your soul."

My gaze lifted from the covered roasting pans and met his. "You mean that was a possibility?"

He nodded, his own eyes far away among those shadowed trees again.

I shook myself and said, "You'd better walk me through it then."

"It's easier to show you."

He uncovered one of the pans and I peered inside, in spite of my dread. It looked like a wet piece of fabric, draped and folded.

"That's not so bad—" I started to say, and then gave a little shriek as I stumbled backwards.

As Lonan lifted the "fabric," it unfurled into a face. The eyes pinched closed and the lips parted slightly, but the movements only accentuated the sense of wrongness of it. Where Lonan's fingers touched the skin directly, it curled around them. Snuggled up like a hairless baby hamster.

"That's...disgusting," I managed. "What the hell is it?"

"It's one of the masks we're going to wear," he paused as he looked at it in THE FACE. "This one's mine and the other's yours."

"No, no, no. What is it even made of? Someone's actual face?"

"That was the modification I made. The original spell did call for a human's face, harvested under great pain and with an awareness of loss. I made a substitution."

It took me a few moments to be able to ask, "So what is that? Someone's happy face instead?"

"No!" He sounded proud and gleeful. "It's chicken skin! From a whole roasting chicken."

His grin told me I was supposed to be impressed by this. "Well, um, good job? But wearing a mask of dead chicken skin doesn't seem like it will be much better than human skin."

That wasn't entirely true—of course it was better some human didn't have to die in "great pain and with an awareness of loss"—but it was still disgusting.

Before I could say anything else, Nykur came running in the kitchen, skidding to a stop on the vinyl flooring. He scowled when he saw Lonan holding up his creation.

"Dammit, I missed it! I wanted to be here when you showed her so I could see the look on *her face.*" He emphasized the last two words and laughed— the same laugh he'd been doing for days.

"You knew what he planned and didn't warn me?" I asked.

"I did," he answered through a chuckle. "I've been asking you if you're going to chicken out, and remember when I said it wasn't too late to save face? I know you heard me say you'd hate the masks he was making."

"Well yeah, but I thought they'd be sloppy papier mache or something. Like, I wouldn't be happy with it, but not that they'd make me want to throw up." Lonan didn't look so proud and gleeful now, so I hastily added, "But it looks like you worked really hard on them, thank you, Lonan."

He still looked a little sulky, so I said, "I mean it, that was really clever to use what we had instead."

And maybe because I was looking for it, I saw his eyes blaze for a moment and a dark shadow spill over him. I also saw the effort he made to get ahold of himself, and that it cost him. I exchanged a look with Nykur.

"I'm sorry," I said, and meant it. "I wasn't taking this seriously—I wasn't taking you seriously—but it does mean a lot to me that you were trying to make the masks less evil, for my sake. Now tell me what to do next."

It turned out most of the magic had already been prepared ahead of time, woven into the masks' creation, so we only had to put them on. Lonan went first so I could see what would happen; the way the skin crawled along his face, like a cephalopod blending into a rocky edifice, creeped me way out.

But then it was like *snap!* and I was looking at someone else's face. Not like a bad movie effect or the "after" photo of a face transplant patient, but an actual whole nother person with sharper cheekbones and a wider mouth. Lonan stretched out his jaw, winked each eye in turn, and grinned at me—it was completely seamless.

"What does it feel like?" I asked. "Does it smell?"

"Once it attaches, you hardly notice it. It's really not that big of a deal."

Lonan New Face watched me, along with Nykur, as I gathered the courage to put on my own mask. The chicken skin hung from my fingers until it heated to my body temperature, and then it flowed around like play slime, sticking and sliding. If I thought about it too much, I was going to completely lose my nerve, so I slapped it onto my face.

The mask flowed over me and I started to panic as my eyes, nose, and mouth were closed off under a film (and it did have a smell, but not too unpleasant). But before I could get a proper panic attack going, everything cleared. I was blinking at Lonan and Nykur, and feeling only like I had put on sunblock a little too thick. The mask moved with me as

I made faces and tested it out, and I let out a sigh of relief.

I tried to see what I looked like in the stainless steel worktop, but the scratches from years of use blurred and warped my reflection. I slid my phone out of my pocket and turned the camera to selfie mode. A different shade of freckles dotted a wider nose than my own, and the shape of the eyes and mouth were completely unlike mine. But my hazel-brown eyes were the same, and my hair hadn't changed—since I was dying it black now instead of red, that probably didn't matter as much to keep me from being recognized.

But the most important thing was that when I looked at my reflection, my Sight didn't tell me anything was wrong. No alarm bells rang in my head, and I wouldn't have looked twice at this person if I'd passed them in the street.

"Well?" Lonan asked.

"You were right, it's not that bad and Nykur was being a dick by trying to freak me out." My forehead creased in unfamiliar wrinkles as I frowned at him, and that made me aware again of the mask. I was already getting used to it.

"Nykur, can you tell we're magicked?" I asked. "With your horse sense, I mean."

He snorted in a very horsey way. "Not really, but then nykurs aren't built to be magical detectors—we're lovers, not filters." That paid me back for my bad joke with a worse one.

Lonan said, "There may be some Fae who can tell there is a spell active, but they shouldn't be able to tell exactly what it is. Any signs could easily be mistaken for a charm to make a wart invisible or something."

"So they might think I'm vain, but they won't leap straight to 'that's Avery Flynn, get her!' if they notice?"

"That's the idea."

"Okay then, we've got our faces, um, covered. Anything else?"

"I'm going to renew the spell for our names, since odds are you'll slip up and call me Lonan in public."

"I've only done that like twice and nobody seemed to notice—"

"What about the times you've referred to yourself as Avery?"

It was better to be safe than Avery while we were out in the world, so I couldn't argue with that. Well, I was tempted to argue because that's just the way I am, but it was true. I still thought of him as Lonan so sometimes that was what came out of my mouth instead of Starling, and I had even more trouble thinking of myself as Cally. I should have picked a cooler name than Calluna, the Latin name for heather, which I'd picked as a reminder of my mom.

The sound of footsteps out in the hall brought me back to the kitchen, and Lonan hastily stowed the evidence of our midnight magics.

Mrs. Shore came in, saying, "What's going on in here? Anything I should know about with a resident?"

But when I turned to her with a smile, she went pale and grabbed the edge of the counter for support. She looked from me to Lonan and her mouth worked as she tried to say something.

"Nykur, catch her!" I cried as she started to collapse in a faint.

He lowered her to the floor and put an apron under her head to pillow it, and when I turned to Lonan to ask what was up, he ducked his head sheepishly.

"There was one other thing I didn't mention. I needed real faces to base the masks on and I didn't want them to be anyone we knew, in case someone else recognized them. So I 'borrowed' the faces from an old photo Mrs. Shore had hanging on her office wall."

It took me a moment to picture the photo he meant, and then I said, "No wonder she fainted! Those are her parents when they were younger, plus they died like twenty years ago."

We really didn't want to burn any bridges with Mrs. Shore, and the three of us decided the best thing was to put her back to bed with a spell to make her think she'd dreamed her parents' faces. But of course that would all go out the window if she saw us again, so it meant we had to leave while she slept.

Here we go, on the run again.

8 Brynn

Mara rescued Brynn from an impending tea party with Riley's toys, saying, "We'd better get going, we still have a lot to do today. Aurora said she'll help us with some business cards, so follow me to the dining room."

As Brynn entered what was obviously no longer used as a dining room, she saw another Fae laboring over a wooden contraption. Or...not another Fae, exactly. There was something off about her—for one thing, most Fae would not have that many tattoos since they could create the same effect with magic.

Sensing Brynn's attention—and the carreg magic reaching for her—the woman looked up and smiled. "I'm Aurora. Dryad halfling, since you're likely wondering."

Ah, that explained her affinity for garden plants from both worlds. It was not unheard of for a union between humans and Fae to produce offspring, but Brynn had certainly never met one; her parents considered them abominations and would likely have killed one on sight. And yet here one was, looking happy and healthy in Mara's house. Proving yet again that her parents had an unnecessarily narrow view of the worlds.

Brynn introduced herself and came closer to see what Aurora was doing. The large machine smelled of rubber and ink, giving Brynn a clue to its function. Within easy reach of its operator, a compartmented box held small metal blocks, neatly organized into the English alphabet. Sheets of paper with a rough, handmade surface waited their turn.

"I've just finished cleaning up from the last job, so I'm nearly ready to go," Aurora said. "What do you want the business cards to say?"

"They talk?" Brynn asked. "Then surely printing is not needed, if they speak for themselves?"

Aurora laughed, not unkindly, and clarified. "These are only small printed cards, with no spells. It's better that way because everyone won't be afraid of it going haywire. They'll last longer, too."

Mara pulled some cards out of her pocket and showed them to Brynn. "Mine say:

Want it? Need it?

Mara's got it, or knows where to get it.

Find her at the Spellmeet Market every after-noon from 1-3.

Got it?"

Brynn read it through herself, checking for any hidden magic but not finding any. "I see. Will my cards make sense?"

"Mine make sense! These fit my customers exactly since they don't have a lot of time to waste, and details about how and where I get stuff can only cause problems."

"What will mine say then?"

Aurora mused, "They should be more professional-sounding than Mara's, as you will have to overcome skepticism. Humans will have never heard of carregs and most Fae will never have met one, with carregs being so rare."

Mara said, "What about 'Vengeance Thwarted' as a business name? With like a graphic of a bloody knife striking a shield made of stone?"

Aurora raised her eyebrows. "Have you been reading Riley's comic books again? We want something more accessible than that. More approachable."

"I did say a *drawing* of a bloody knife," Mara muttered. "It can be cartoony and fun."

Ignoring her, Aurora said, "I was thinking more along the lines of:

CARREG FOR HIRE
Curses lifted
Spells undone
Non-magical items restored
Results guaranteed, at a reasonable fee."

Mara made a face. "At least let me do a logo for it."

"As long as you can come up with something in the time it takes to lay out the type and prep the ink roller."

With that time limit, Mara and Riley both bent their heads over a paper as they drafted possible logos.

It turned out Aurora did not work alone; a crew of pixies scampered along the type trays, gathering the correct letters and dropping them into place. The pixies knew their business and got the job done with little of their usual mischief.

Riley and Mara would not let Brynn see their design until they felt it was ready, and they proudly brought over their artwork. It featured a female figure, silhouetted with hands on hips in a confident posture, on a jagged mountain top and with lightning bolts coming out of the sky.

Brynn had to smile; it definitely would have been right at home in one of the comic books that had lain open in Riley's bedroom. Especially if they used different colored ink to pick out the details, it was a logo to make a carreg proud. Except for one thing...

"Could you make her standing on a hill instead of a mountain?"

Riley argued, "But mountains are bigger and stronger—" before Mara hushed her. Mara's grin showed she knew Brynn was trying to turn the insulting name her parents had given her into a strength.

"Good thinking," Mara said.

The pixies got to work carving a slab of rubber with the reversed logo, for making a stamp of the design. The wooden press printed the text with black ink onto a large, heavy sheet of paper before one of the pixies strapped blades to her feet and skated across the surface. The scoring allowed the cards to separate easily, and then Riley inked the rubber stamp and carefully lined up the logo on each one.

In no time, Brynn was holding her very own business cards in her hands. She touched the logo with a smile, and noticed the contact details were the same as Mara's. Brynn guessed if the usual messaging methods (whether magic or technical) did not work, then it was best to set up business hours like this. Plus, at least Mara would be around to help her with questions. If it also meant she got to spend a few hours every day with Mara, how could Brynn complain?

On her insistence, Mara let Brynn pedal the rickshaw while she and Riley made chauffeur jokes in the back. But after the initial excitement wore off, Brynn regretted her choice. Her muscles felt like they had been hit with a fire spell, and soon she was gasping like a water sprite on shore.

After their first stop to deliver some of Aurora's potions to a "drug store," Mara took up the pedaling again without being asked.

Brynn said, "That looks so much easier than it is! Thank you for letting me try, but I believe I'll need to work up to longer stretches. Apparently the life of a Fae lady did not keep me as fit as I thought."

"Didn't you have sweeping staircases in your castle? And long galleries of portraits to walk in your flowing dresses?" Mara asked.

Brynn laughed because under the veneer of mockery, she detected a longing from Mara that was almost equal to Riley's desire for unicorns. Did she secretly long to be pampered royalty? If so, Brynn could only offer her own reality.

"The stairs were more for architectural beauty and status than for real use. There were discreet alcoves with traveling spells for the human servants' use, and my own, since we could not magick ourselves to different parts of the castle like the real Fae could."

Mara shot a curious glance over her shoulder. "Aren't you real Fae?"

Brynn let out a rueful laugh. "It depends on whom you ask. My bloodlines are pure and I was treasured as a child—until my carreg powers showed themselves. Then I learned not to remind my parents of my existence, or they would take out their shame on the daughter who not only could not do spells and charms, but whose only function was to undermine the magic of real Fae."

Mara slowed her pedaling and was about to say something further, but Riley piped up with, "You can't do spells and charms? Not any?"

"No, Little One. Not even the smallest of them. What about you?"

Riley launched into a list of the charms she knew, and what could have been a sad moment passed. But Mara must have thought Brynn needed cheering up because instead of their next planned stop, the rickshaw pulled up in front of a hair salon.

What was supposed to be a quick stop to dye Brynn's hair turned into Riley spying a new nail polish, and Mara trying out some new cosmetics. So Brynn came away with purple ombre hair, and smoky cat eyes and sparkly fingernails like her companions. When Riley got sleepy after the excitement and snuggled up to her in the rickshaw, Brynn let her do it and slipped an arm around her. Mara rewarded her with a dazzling smile and Brynn made a note to do more things to make her friend happy.

It almost made Brynn forget how flirty Mara had been with the employees in the salon.

After a quick bite to eat at a coffee place, where they left one of Brynn's cards on a bulletin board, they headed to a repair shop so Mara could drop off her toaster. Mara said Brynn could stay outside if the metal bothered her, but Brynn said, "Mountains have a lot of metal in them, you know. It does not bother me that much."

The truth was, the Fae sensitivity to metal was part of the old Border spell, another way to restrict the movements of creatures in the human world. But the Fae had let the humans continue to believe metal was protection against them because it often worked in their favor (like how the sanguinary Fae who inspired the vampire myths actually love garlic). Humans got complacent with their precautions if they thought a horseshoe—or a braid of odiferous cloves—over the door was enough to keep them safe.

Brynn gasped in delight when they entered the repair shop, taking in the jumble of parts filling every surface. Innards of countless devices even hung from the ceiling, whether as decoration or sales stock Brynn could not tell. Oil and rust competed for her nose's attention, nearly making her sneeze. She could not have imagined a more enchanting place—but enchanting was not the right word, was it? Prosaic was a better fit, perhaps. The opposite of a magical workplace, where spells conjured items to order.

A few magical gadgets mixed in also chimed to her aural senses. She reached out and ran her fingers along a gleaming chrome circle, with spokes woven from the center to outer rim. Maybe it was a wheel? Or art to hang on a wall?

Brynn startled at Mara's laugh, and smiled back at her uncertainly. "What?"

"I've never seen a Fae go so nerdy. You look like my cousin when she lines up to buy the next hot video game."

The mention of family made Brynn think of her own and her enjoyment of the shop dimmed a little. But she wondered how mockery from Mara could make her feel closer, like they were becoming real friends, as opposed to when her family tried to tear Brynn down with their words.

Following a narrow path through the clutter, Brynn was startled to come upon a human working at a table at the back of the store. A vest covered with discs with sayings like "Powered by Wind" and "Every Day is Taco Day" caught Brynn's eye, but the important tag seemed to be the one that said "Taylor—they/them."

While deep in concentration, the tip of Taylor's tongue extended from one corner of their mouth as they struggled to tighten one piece while simultaneously holding two parts together. Without being asked, Brynn reached out to hold the parts tight, freeing up the person's other hand so they could work more freely.

"Thanks," they said, wiping a smear of grease across their cheek as they pushed their hair out of their face. "That was one stubborn nut."

Brynn took a closer look; was this a hybrid device that used natural parts like tree nuts, as well as metal?

The human saw her interest and named off several pieces in the hand vac's interior before closing it up. When they pressed a switch, a roar like a miniature griffin came out of it and apparently that was correct.

"There you are, Taylor," Mara said as she emerged from another aisle. She must have picked up on something between Brynn and the shopkeeper, because she leaned in to Taylor. "Am I interrupting anything?"

Mara's voice purred with flirtation but Taylor rolled their eyes. "What now, Mara? I'm interviewing a possible apprentice."

Brynn looked around, expecting to see someone behind her.

Taylor chuckled and said, "You. I meant you. Do you want the job?"

Before Brynn could answer, Mara said, "You can't have her, she's mine."

As both Brynn and Taylor turned their startled gazes to her, Mara stuttered, "I mean, I've already set her up with some jobs. She's working on fixing magical problems. Brynn's a carreg."

"Care to translate that?" Taylor asked Brynn.

"I am a carreg, a type of Fae who restores things to their rightful states." Brynn handed Taylor a card. "I have already gotten Mara's toaster to stop singing, so she brought it to you to fix the heating element, I think?" That was a nice touch, to impress Taylor with some technology words.

Mara placed her toaster on a clear space on the table and said, "Yeah. It still burns my toast."

As if Mara had not spoken, Taylor asked, "Restores things to their rightful states? Like fixing them? If you can do that with magical items, we'd make a great team. Sure you don't want to join my shop?"

Brynn started to answer, but hesitated. She did want to learn more about fixing mechanical devices, but did not want to seem ungrateful to Mara. "Could I not work with both of you?"

Now Taylor was the awkward one. "I can't afford to spend my time teaching you if it's not going to benefit my business in the long run. I'm sorry."

Mara perked up at the hint of a negotiation, seeming to forget that she was the one who had been discouraging Brynn before. "But Brynn can fix the magical stuff that comes through here—you'd hate to miss out on that, right?"

"Well...I don't know how much magical stuff I actually get in here—"

"I counted five magical items as I walked through your shop," Brynn interrupted. "And that was only one aisle."

Taylor's eyebrow piercing bobbed in surprise. "Really? Show me."

9 Brynn

Brynn led them to the nearest object, pointing to a metal thing with a cord curled around it. The humans peered at it but did not touch it.

"What is it?" Mara asked.

Taylor answered, "Mechanically, it's a hair straightener. What else is it, Brynn?"

Brynn tilted her head to one side as she tried to tune her aural senses into it. "It is not—it does not seem harmful. The spell makes it..."

She trailed off as she considered. "Would a spell to make hair turn multi-colored make sense? That seems silly."

But Mara's eyes lit up. "No, that would be great. Somebody must have paid to have this spell added and then the straighteners ended up here. I wonder why—" Mara cut herself off, as the most likely reason the appliance had ended up here was the owner fell on hard times, or worse.

"So this isn't one of those tricky spells that gives rainbow hair but also makes the human crave pigeon blood or something weird?" Taylor asked.

Brynn checked again before answering, "No, it really is only for rainbow hair. It is likely that the person will have multi-colored hair until a carreg or someone else cancels it out, but no more harm than that. Have there been a lot of spells which cause humans to crave pigeon blood?"

"Once was enough," Taylor said without explaining more. "What other magical objects do I have lurking in my store, Brynn?"

Brynn followed her aural senses to a handful of other bespelled items in the same aisle; most were harmless magic but one would have caused some serious boils to the person who put on the headphones. To be safe, Taylor asked Brynn to cancel out the spells; they would rather make a sure sale with a safe object than risk the spells backfiring.

She did as they asked and then, inspired by Mara's bargaining, Brynn said, "I would like to learn about human technology too. Perhaps you could show me how to fix the toaster?"

Taylor agreed and since it was not a very complicated device, the lesson and the repairs were finished in time for Brynn and Mara to head to the market for their advertised business hours.

The marketplace was another feast for Brynn's senses, which she had not realized were quite so starved from her years of confinement to her family's castle. For her, the cacophony of so many different creatures and humans sharing a relatively small square was underlaid by the blaring of spells and magic. Just as the colorful, patchwork dresses described as "boho chic" at one booth caught her eye, her aural senses reveled in the interweaving of the melodies of so many magical novelties.

Mara told her the place used to be a mini-golf, whatever that was. The shabby windmills, giant lizards, and worn green "grass" must have been original, from before the booths and stores sprang up between them like mushrooms. Mature trees pooled shade and attracted children to climb in their branches.

Food vendors clustered together at one end of the row, and one of the mismatched table and chair sets served as Mara's office. She held court there to a steady stream of customers, some in search of items—in which case, Mara made arrangements to deliver the item on another trip, or sent them to someone who had the item—and others stopping by to pick something up or to chat.

Mara seemed well-liked, despite flirting shamelessly with everyone. But as Brynn listened, she noticed Mara's banter was not as shallow as it seemed—she ferreted out little details on who was harvesting their garden right now and might have vegetables to spare, or who was leaving Spellmeet and might have some household goods to clear out. And who might need them.

Her easy conversations were actually the foundation for her business of matching supply with demand, and most people seemed to know but played along. After all, they would likely benefit in some way themselves someday.

Mara introduced Brynn to each person, pulling her into the circle of friends and associates. A few people made appointments for Brynn to come consult on a spell or curse, but most met her with polite skepticism. It was more wearying than Brynn expected and Mara suggested that Brynn could explore the rest of the market—as long as she handed out her cards along the way.

Brynn started with the food booths, drawn by the enticing smells. Fortunately there was not a tuna salad sandwich in sight, and the samples of funnel cake and cinnamon rolls proved delightful. She traded a few coins (from a stash in her apartment) for a cinnamon roll larger than her head and peeled off sections as she walked along.

Most of the booths featured secondhand garb or home goods, but a few sported bolts of fabric or other supplies for making your own clothing. There were several book stalls and Brynn was tempted to lay more coins down for those, but remembered she would have access to Mrs. Dibbs's library and it would be a waste to buy some titles now.

She stopped again to look at stacked cages filled with animals. Were they meant for food or as pets? They seemed well cared for and the proprietor made clucking noises as he fed bits of meat through the bars so perhaps pets? Unless he was fattening them up. She passed over the rabbits and birds in favor of the cats, stopping in front of one placid tortoiseshell.

"If you want a lap cat, that one is perfect," the caretaker said. "She'll keep you warm in winter and warmer in summer. And I got her spayed a few weeks ago, so no worries about finding homes for kittens."

"What is spayed?" Brynn asked.

He frowned, not sure if she was joking. "The vet takes out their reproductive organs so they can't breed. It helps with overpopulation."

Now Brynn frowned. "Do they also do this with humans?"

His lips thinned as her words clued him in that she herself was not human. "Of course not. That would be wrong."

"Oh, then I am afraid this—this one has been wronged. May I?" She gestured to the cage's latch.

"Are you going to buy her?"

"If that's what it takes." Brynn handed him some of the paper money and he seemed satisfied at the amount.

Taking the cat gently from its cage, Brynn set her on the pavement and stretched out her aural senses. Before the man's startled eyes, the tortoiseshell cat turned into a bedraggled young woman crouched on the ground. With a wild look in her eyes, she scrambled on all fours back towards her cage, and when she failed to fit inside she tried to leap on top of the stack.

Falling far short, the woman lay there panting.

"Is that Kaylen? Kaylen Strong?" the man asked in a soft voice.

The young woman slanted her eyes in his direction and a sob escaped her. He spoke soothingly to her as he helped her to her feet, and after getting her bearings she was able to walk over to a chair. A few others exclaimed over her and soon she was sipping a cup of tea, surrounded by well-wishers also calling her Kaylen.

When the boothman returned to her, Brynn asked, "Who is she?"

"She was one of my students. I used to teach high school biology and Kaylen disappeared a year ago—some said she ran away, but it wasn't like her. Has she been a cat this entire time?"

"I cannot say. All I know is she was cursed into cat shape; it was not something she asked for."

"Thank you for helping her." He started to turn back to Kaylen but then faced Brynn again. "You paid for a cat, do you want to pick another one? And I'll send some cat food with you in thanks."

Brynn started to say no thank you but paused outside a cage with a sleek black cat inside. It pressed into the back of the cage and hissed at her, ears slanted evilly.

"That one is a barn cat, he's not tame at all. Wouldn't you rather have a nice kitty?"

Brynn poked one finger through the wire and the cat slashed at her but did not make contact. She could tell this one was not enchanted, merely wild and undeserving of confinement in a cage. "No, I want this one please."

The man reached under a table for a box.

"That won't be necessary," Brynn said, and un-latched the cage.

"Wait—" But the cat had already streaked through the open door and between the feet of the passing crowd, losing itself in the distance. Perhaps it would find refuge in Mara's garden colony.

Brynn smiled to see it free and she and the man shook hands, their business concluded. She returned to Mara's table in time to help her pack up a few things and jump in the rickshaw.

They stopped at Mara's house first and joined the residents for dinner, a chaotic meal where dishes of food covered a sideboard. People came through and filled their plates and took them to their rooms if they wanted solitude, or out in the garden if they wanted company and nature.

Brynn sampled all the Fae recipes, as well as the human dishes Riley recommended (they seemed to have similar preferences for sweets vs. savories). At first, Brynn held back and merely eavesdropped on the lively conversations swirling around her—but Mara would not let her get away with that for long and dragged Aurora over to sit beside her.

Aurora said, "I hear you restored a girl from cat form today? And released a hissy little black cat to the streets."

"I did." Brynn was not sure which of the two she was prouder of.

"Well, word's getting around about what you did for Kaylen," Aurora said, "so don't be surprised if you get more business now."

Aurora proved to be correct, and Brynn was busy over the next few weeks with calls on her carreg powers: she removed a curse that caused toads to spill from a young girl's mouth when she spoke (so old school, as Mara put it), she released a troll from the geis keeping him beneath a bridge, and she restored a series of magicked shoes to merely regular shoes. Apparently it had been a fad for humans to get their shoes enchanted for dancing, but no one had thought to include a command to make them stop, so quite a few people had shoes tapping in their closets.

Whenever she could, Brynn stopped by Taylor's shop and lost herself in the glorious madness of the machines. She still was barely at the apprentice level, but at least she did not embarrass herself by handing Taylor an electric toothbrush when they had asked for a soldering iron. Or at least, not after the first time it happened.

Her life would have been perfect, if not for Brynn's frustrations over Mara's mixing of signals. The two of them were so often in each other's company while also part of a crowd: at the market, at Mara's house, at a café, Brynn seemed to be always in Mara's orbit but could not get any closer. Mara flirted back with everyone but Brynn—Brynn's attempts at overt flirting were met with wide-eyed stammering and a quick exit from Mara. And yet, if Brynn showed the slightest interest in anyone else, Mara appeared and found some way to divert attention back to herself.

After the time Mara showed up earlier than usual at Brynn's apartment and found a human male eating his breakfast while Brynn showered, the look in Mara's eyes meant Brynn had not repeated the undertaking. Or was Mara's disapproval because she did not think Fae and human relationships could work, a sentiment she had mentioned several times?

Mara had made a few snide comments until Brynn asked her outright, "Are you more upset I was with a human male or that it was not you eating breakfast after a night of passion?"

But Mara had just laughed it off—"a night of passion? Are you in an 80s soap opera?"—and pretended Brynn had never asked. Humans were terribly confusing, and Brynn did not find the courage to ask about Mara's feelings so bluntly again. Instead, she dove into work and enjoyed her other relationships with Taylor and Riley and Aurora, plus new friends she made every day.

Her apartment became a sanctuary at the end of a long day, embracing her with a calming quiet. She would not have invited strangers over at that point anyway (even if Mara had not reacted so badly to discovering Brynn had a sex life), because it was her space alone. It felt almost as much a home as her mountain did, and for an oread that said a lot.

10 Avery

I hadn't realized how trapped I'd felt by Shady Grove's walls until we were on the road again. Okay, so it wasn't the walls which had trapped me so much as it was the chance of getting caught by someone who hated me. Who, again, was pretty much every human and Fae creature still in existence. But while wearing this face and some preppy clothes from the lost and found I'd otherwise never touch, I could stride down the asphalt without fear.

So I did, Avery-style.

I twirled and yodeled, skipped and shouted, jigged and whistled. If my old friend Daniel had been with me, he would have been mortified and walked far enough ahead or behind me so people wouldn't think we were together. But he was in Faerie with his parents, and Lonan was enough of a clown to join in. We finished off with a rousing version of the hokey-pokey, both of us giddy and flushed.

Then we came to the highway, and a cacophony of sound nearly overwhelmed me. The two lanes in either direction had been restriped to allow a lane for cars, a lane for animal-powered vehicles or riders, and for the foot traffic trudging along the shoulder. Snippets of news I'd heard came back to me: sections of the highway had gone missing during the Shifting, or had had a hill plonked down in the middle of them, and traveling was no longer so straightforward. Transportation these days was a patchwork of motorized buses, animal-drawn vehicles, cars that ran on gas, magic, or a hybrid of the two—and of course, by foot.

Trains and planes were out of favor, for various dragon-related reasons. I hadn't believed it when Lonan had told me that howdahs on the backs of giant caterpillars had become common, but sure enough there were several in sight. *How big is the moth or butterfly those caterpillars turn into?* I shuddered and went back to scanning the crowds.

After being isolated with a small group of people for so long, however close we'd become, I didn't even know how to process it all. My Sight went into overdrive, fixating on breaks in the pattern that read as "wrong." Like the hulking man riding a horse that flickered and showed itself to be a centaur instead, glamoured to blend in. But then an entire family of centaurs passed in the riders' lane, so what was the point of that specific centaur disguising himself? Maybe to get through a checkpoint, but everyone knew Sighted humans had steady work at the waystations and would spot that easily.

Most glamours and spells I detected were smaller things, like a change in hair color or a charm to turn away malicious intent. There must be a booming business in magical items, as well as the low-tech hand carts and bicycles which seemed to be everywhere. At a roadside stand, you could even buy coffee with a quickening spell added—which struck me as redundant. *But I bet the soccer moms are total addicts—if there are still soccer moms.*

"What do you think?" Lonan's question brought my focus back to him. "Should we walk or catch a caterpillar or something?"

"Wait, explain something to me first—how did all this get here? I mean, the Shifting ended less than a year ago and no way did an entire new system grow overnight."

"Parts of the infrastructure literally did grow overnight." Lonan loved a chance to be smug about knowing something I didn't. "But most of this is here because some entrepreneurs and inventors took advantage of the time differences in pockets of Faerie. They could duck into one and take all the time they needed to come up with a workable design and start production on the magical parts. Then they'd pop back out and pick up with the technology, and Hob's your uncle."

"The saying is 'Bob's your uncle'," I argued.

"Not where I'm from. So, do we take a caterpillar or not?"

"It already feels like my personal bubble is being infringed on, so I think a caterpillar or bus would be too much right now. What about your shapeshifting? Can't you turn into a big ol' crow with a saddle on it?"

He shook his head and said in a low voice, "Shifting will pop this mask right off. I made it for my humanoid form so that's the only one it will work for. Plus, you sound so lazy and spoiled right now. If I could shift, I'd totally be a regular-sized crow and ride on your shoulder while you walk."

"You're right, my entitlement was showing." I laughed through my blush. "Guess you'll miss out on all the bad jokes you know you want to make about me 'riding you for hours'."

We agreed to rent bikes and it turned out to be a good way for me to adjust to the crowds. The physical effort meant I wasn't completely caught up in my head, and the speed of our travel meant I didn't have to be near any one instance of glamour long enough for it to really bother me. Instead of the crowd pressuring my senses, I shared a sense of camaraderie with my fellow travelers.

For the most part, that seemed to be the case with everyone. Traffic flowed smoothly and points of conflict dissolved as the cart drivers and faster riders accommodated each other, while cyclists took advantage of gaps to pass them both with a cheery wave. It was like ballet set to an unheard music, a perfect harmony of movement working towards the same goal.

*In fact, it was too perfect...*if I squinted right, a shimmering magic overlaid the pavement, flowing along and pulling the travelers with it.

"Hey, Lo—Starling," I called to my companion. "Is it my imagination or is this road magicked for happy travelers?"

"Yeah, this section is. When we rented these bikes, it was like checking an 'I agree to the TOS' box on a webpage. We have to abide by the spell if we want to ride here. Not all the roads have it, but if you're rich enough you can hire wyvern guards to get you safely through the other sections."

I snorted. "Who trusts wyverns? Not me."

"A lot of people do; the biggest startup is Phoenix Rising. It's not too far off from the tradition of hiring wyverns as mercenaries—and they only rarely eat the drivers or passengers these days."

"How comforting."

I had more snark in me, but we hit a hill and I saved my breath for pedaling. By about the third hill, bicycling had lost its charm for sure. The rest of the afternoon was a blur of screaming leg muscles and a growling stomach, until we finally pulled off as the sun went down. The magic of the road was now visible as a helpful glow to illuminate the way overnight, but I was done.

We got a room in a roadside inn, a converted Motel 6. The rooms were the same (even the '80s décor) but a stable covered half the parking lot, housing animals and lesser Fae creatures alike. I thought back to the centaurs I'd seen and wondered whether they took a room or a stable? And would it be racist/species-ist to ask?

Once we were in our room, I hobbled over to the bed and collapsed onto the stale sheets while Lonan went to find us some food (see my aforementioned lazy and spoiled qualities). After inhaling a carton of mystery-meat stew and half a dozen rolls, I groaned, "How much further is it to Spellmeet? Are we really going to be bicycling for days?"

"It's still faster and easier than walking. And you're the one who left Nykur behind. We could have spent our time writhing together in the back seat instead—"

I drowned out the rest of his words with a dramatic sigh and then added, "Don't you know any other nykurs? Or have some favors to call in?"

"Not any that wouldn't draw attention to me. How about a hot bath and one of my 'special' massages?"

His eyebrow waggle made it clear he expected the massage to end happily, but it's not like that was a hardship for me—not once his magical hands eased all the soreness out of my muscles. I flopped over on the bed so he could start on my back and let the magic flow over me—*aaah*.

Those massages were the only thing that kept me going over the next several days and nights. We hopped off our bikes when the magicked road section ended and rode on a caterpillar for a while—which was nice because at least we were sitting without pedaling. But then we had to ride in the back of a covered wagon, pulled by a woolly green rhino, as part of a caravan. All the wyvern outriders made me jumpy and it took me a while to believe they weren't going to recognize me somehow.

Finally, we arrived at the outer checkpoint for Spellmeet, staffed by Sighted humans and Fae civil servants. Passing their scrutiny is what made me have faith in our masks at last and I breathed a sigh of relief as we walked into town.

"Where do we go first?" Lonan asked, but before I could answer he added in a falsetto, "Food! I'm starving!"

I punched him in the arm for mocking me, but my feet were already steering us to a row of booths set up by the roadside. With a gasp, I ran up to the one selling pasties and joined the line.

"Um, I think I'll pass on the bogshroom and enchanted hart flavors," I whispered to Lonan. "Do you think I'd be safe with the cheese, broccoli, and sparkpotato pasty?"

"The question is, will the rest of us be safe with you eating that explosive combo?" he shout-whispered back.

I ignored him and asked, "What is a sparkpotato, anyway? It sounds like a badly translated snack from Japan."

"It's an enchanted tuber some Brownie created centuries ago from human potatoes. It's perfect for living rough—the peelings self-combust, once you peel it. You cook the starchy part right in their fire. Watch."

Sure enough, the cook used a slotted spoon to retrieve what looked like potato peelings from a tub of water. As the water drained away, the peelings started steaming. Once he added them to the ceramic box below the cooktop, the flames leapt up.

"That's pretty damn clever," I commented. "But they're safe for humans to eat? And they're real food, not some glamoured trick?"

"What does your Sight tell you?"

"Nothing, so I guess I'm good to eat it." I happily collected my pasties and bit into the first one as we walked.

The booths got thicker as we got closer to the gates into Spellmeet proper, lining the road in an unbroken row of carnival mood. Some dealt strictly in human tech and supplies, like phone chargers and snack foods, and a few others were so full of Fae charms they looked like a psychedelic music video to my Sighted eyes.

But the ones I lingered at were those which had combined human objects and Fae magic in clever ways. Like knockoff brands of human candy: Footsie Roll pops that made your feet feel like they'd just had a spa day, pairs of red wax lips turned into short-distance communicators, or Smarmies to help you flatter someone effectively.

By the time we hit the final checkpoint that would let us into Spellmeet, bags and packages weighed me down. Lonan sported a tall hat with a cuckoo bird who shot out at random times and hollered insults at passersby.

"You smell like you're hiding a compost pile under that skirt!" it yelled at a dryad, whose leafy hair wilted in hurt.

"Did your momma win all the ugly contests, until you came along and took the crowns?" That was to a guard at the gate, who really did look like a troll under the plastic *Frozen* tiara glued to their helmet.

The guard snatched the hat off Lonan's head and twisted it between their huge hands—I didn't think even a magic insult bird could survive that. Lonan took his sad sack hat and perched it on his head defiantly.

"Hey, he spent good money on that hat," I protested. "He should be reimbursed."

"That so?" one of the other guards grumbled. "He wouldn't have been able to take it into Spellmeet anyway, an unstable spell like that. What other contraband do you have in those bags?"

Before I could protest, both guards rifled through my purchases. "Hey! Not my bag of Footsie Pops—I was going to eat those tonight!"

But they didn't care and confiscated everything else we'd bought in the bazaar. Lonan elbowed me so many times, as a reminder not to make a scene, that I was sure my ribs would be blooming with bruises later.

"Tourist dreck," the guard said as they pitched my purchases into a trash can. "Only the ones who won't actually risk going into Spellmeet buy this garbage."

I muttered, "But it's *our* garbage," as they let us through the checkpoint with the rest of our belongings. Still, the effort of holding my tongue had tired me out, so we headed straight to the food court of the Spellmeet market. Not only because I was hungry again, but because I knew Missa would be there at this time of day.

In one of her messages, she'd mentioned she had "office hours" every afternoon, at the table under a jacaranda tree. But as we approached, Missa wasn't there—instead, a Fae seemed to be helping some customers.

Lonan and I exchanged looks, and his raised eyebrow communicated, "See, this is why we needed a plan. What now?"

"Why don't you get us each a cup of tea—ooo, and get me one of those peanut butter and jellyfungus cookies they have—and I'll get us a table while we do some reconnaissance," I said.

He rolled his eyes but went to stand in line. I chose a table close enough to hear what the Fae said, but on the fringes of the food court in case we needed to leave suddenly.

The Fae was dressed in a bizarre outfit of mismatched pieces, but really it wasn't any stranger than any others I'd seen. She seemed to be nervous—or maybe unsure—as she sat at what should be Missa's table.

As I watched, a pair of humans approached the Fae and asked, "You're the carreg?"

"Yes, I'm Brynn, what can I help you with?" she answered in a musical voice.

The boy spoke, but his words were garbled and incomprehensible. He clenched his hands in frustration, until the woman placed a calming hand on his arms.

"He made a bad wish," she said.

The boy tried to say something else, but the woman talked over him. "He would say the wish was fine, but the wish peddler tricked him. I told him that's what Fae do and he should have known better."

The woman remembered she was talking to a Fae and the color bleached from her face. "I mean, probably not you, my lady, you are honorable, I'm sure—"

Brynn waved her hasty apology aside and said, "No offense taken. What did he wish for?"

"To be able to understand all spoken languages, including human, animal, and Fae. He put a lot of thought into phrasing his wish and thought he had it figured out.

"My son is clever, but apparently not as clever as he thinks."

The boy let out a series of guttural cries and high-pitched chirps and Brynn smiled sadly.

"Let me guess," she asked, "he failed to stipulate that he also be understood in those languages?"

The boy hung his head as the woman answered for him. "Yes, that's it exactly. Can you help him?"

Lonan deposited a mug of tea in front of me and joined me in eavesdropping.

11 Brynn

Brynn studied the play of aural magic around the boy whose wish had gone wrong. She had never seen a spell quite like this, with different-colored tendrils wrapping him head to toe. They lay thicker where his mouth was, twisting and tangling when he tried to speak.

"I can help him by removing the spell altogether, but he will lose the abilities he bargained for. I am afraid there is no halfway measure for this cure."

The boy shook his head vigorously, making sharp cutting motions with his hands—apparently the spell's twist did not affect communication with gestures. With a sigh, his mother drew him aside to argue with him. Their voices rose in volume, with the boy's attempts at speech hurting Brynn's ears, until finally the woman dragged him back to the table.

"I want you to take the spell off," she told Brynn. "He's only a boy and has his entire life ahead of him."

Brynn went and kneeled before the boy, looking him in the eyes. They swam with tears, and desperately pleaded with Brynn not to take away his wish.

"If I do this, he will never forgive you," she warned his mother.

"Of course he'll forgive me eventually—I'm his mother." But the woman did not sound half as sure as her words.

Brynn looked back to the child, who now drooped with defeat and she asked, "Is your main issue that he cannot speak with you? Or with others?"

Now the woman let her fear show. "He can't go through life like this. And there's no reason for him to make things harder for himself—I want him to have a good life."

Did this woman not know that many others do indeed have a good life, in spite of whether they can speak or hear? Brynn stood and said, "I will make you a deal. If you will take him to the community center on Tuesday afternoon, you will find a girl named Freya there. She teaches sign language to anyone who wants to learn, for a reasonable fee.

"If your son takes lessons for a few months but they don't work out—and you still want me to remove the spell—then I will do so."

The woman bit her lip, torn as she looked at her son who clenched her hand tightly in hope. "Then I might be out the money for the lessons and for the cost of removing the spell. I think it would be better to do it now."

Brynn sighed. "Fine, if you still want me to remove the spell in two months' time, I will do it at no charge. But I will check with Freya—or whomever you choose to instruct your son—to see you are giving the lessons a genuine chance.

"Do we have a deal?"

After a suspenseful few moments, the woman nodded reluctantly and the boy tore off into the crowd, with whooping cries that startled the birds from the trees. Brynn smiled to herself and turned back to the table.

She stopped as she caught a couple nearby staring intently at her; once they realized she had caught them, they focused on the cookies and tea before them and pretended they had not been watching her. Something about them caught Brynn's attention—were they ensorcelled? Her attempt to reach out with her aural magic did not seem to show anything worrying from this distance.

The more likely explanation was they needed her help and were getting up the courage to approach her. That was happening more frequently as word got around of her successes, but humans were still wary of whether a Fae could—or would—actually help them without also including a trick or a surprise debt to be paid later.

Brynn sat at the table and tried to look unintimidating. But while a few other humans and Fae stopped by to get spells reverted, or to make appointments for her to come to another address on another date, that couple stayed where they were.

Eventually, Mara came back to their "office" and joined Brynn.

"Sorry I was gone so long," Mara said. "I had only agreed to arrange delivery of some new furniture at the restaurant, but of course no one was there when I met the truck. So I had to help unload the tables and chairs; fortunately the driver was part orc so he did all the big stuff.

"Anyway, I'm glad all we have planned for tonight is to watch *The Princess Bride* and eat junk food at your place. Especially since Aurora is watching Riley—that kid has every line memorized and whisper-shouts them through the whole mov-ie."

Brynn had been looking forward to the evening too, mainly because it was a chance for them to be alone together. She had begun to hope Mara might make a move during one of their movie nights—or that she would at least make it clearer she wel-comed such a move from Brynn.

"Will you want any snacks from the food court?" Brynn asked. "I noticed those cheesy pastry things you like are getting low at Willow's stand—"

A throat clearing nearby interrupted Brynn, and Mara and she both turned to look. It was the couple who had been watching Brynn earlier, but now they were focused on Mara.

"I hear you can get anything for us," the girl whispered. "Is that true?"

Brynn frowned; the girl's secretive manner was belied by the sparkle of suppressed mischief in her eyes. Plus, there was something odd about their faces—if Brynn focused her aural senses on them, her magic slid right off. It could not get a fix on them.

Brynn opened her mouth to ask them a few questions, but Mara was already speaking.

"Yes, I can get almost anything within reason and within safety. What did you have in mind?"

The girl looked to her companion and he glanced around furtively before saying, "She has a thing for...feet. And socks, the stinkier the better."

The girl's elbow lashed out at him but she did not deny his statement. If anything, the indignant poke prodded him to escalate his request.

"We were wondering, could you get her some socks from a troll? The kind with such rancid feet that toestools grow on them?

"They make her all...sensual, if you know what I mean."

He waggled his eyebrows suggestively, in case he was being too subtle for them.

Mara kept her expression carefully neutral while she said, "Um, I might be able to arrange that. Is this an, er, urgent matter?"

The two answered at the same moment, with the girl saying, "No," and the boy saying, "Yes." The girl glared at him and he patted her shoulder with great care.

"Now, Picklepuss, if you don't get your next batch of socks soon, you'll have to slake your lust some other way. You might even go so far as to lie with a person with an unfortunate tramp stamp. What makes a girl get a tattoo on her lower back that says 'Exit Only' anyway? There's got to be a story there."

Brynn thought this was a strange aside, but the words made Mara go very still suddenly. She looked at the pair with narrowed eyes. Brynn was glad Mara had finally picked up on something off about these two.

"What an oddly specific thing to say," Mara said, all forced casualness. "I don't think I caught your names. Who are you again?"

The girl snickered before saying, "I'm Cally and this is Starling."

Mara nodded and asked, "No last name?"

The girl looked around furtively before whispering, "Momsicle."

The nonsensical word had a transformative effect on Mara. Suddenly, she was grinning from ear to ear and hugging Cally and Starling, incoherent as she babbled joyfully. Mara's long hugs looked like she knew them—and her hand placement made it look like she knew them intimately.

Now the Cally person and Mara were both babbling again, talking over each other but still somehow in a conversation. Like old friends, the kind who could pick up with each other as if no time had passed apart. So why had Mara never mentioned this Cally and Starling to Brynn, if they were such a part of her past?

Jealousy welled up in Brynn until she blurted, "You know this foot lover, Mara?"

The other three turned startled eyes on Brynn.

"Foot lover?" the girl asked blankly. "Oh, that's Starling's weird sense of humor. I just told him 'let's have some fun with Mara' and that's what he came up with."

Jarring notes of magic grated on Brynn as the girl spoke their names. Brynn frowned and asked, "What should I call you, please, if you do not prefer Picklepuss?"

"Cally is fine," the girl said, and this time it sounded normal to both Brynn's ears and her aural senses. Brynn would need to keep an ear out to see if there was a pattern to the alarms. Unless it was a coincidence that some disharmonious magic intruded when Cally was speaking before?

But it was not coincidence when Brynn still could not get a fix on their faces as Mara's friends joined them at the table. Brynn relaxed her senses and tried to slide sideways onto their features, as if she could catch some spell unawares. But every time, their faces flickered like the old movies played on TV late at night. Still the same face, but it did not fit with the rest of their bodies.

And throughout their conversation with Mara, the discordant magic would hit Brynn when Cally spoke. Only when she said names, and not every single time. It was like some spell overrode her speech and changed what the listener heard. For Brynn, it was like a blast of white noise and then the names "Cally" and "Starling" and sometimes even for "Mara." Why would a spell be affecting Mara's name? It was what everyone called her.

Annoyance and jealousy made Brynn's coffee taste stale while the others talked. Finally, Mara stood and exclaimed, "Okay, office hours are over. Let's get out of here."

Brynn also stood and gathered her things, asking, "Do you want to stop and get some cheesy pastries on the way then or not?"

Mara cocked her head, distracted by Cally and Starling's antics as they tried to throw their trash into the can from fifty feet away.

"On the way?" Mara asked. "Oh—the movie night. Can we do a raincheck? I haven't seen these two in ages."

Brynn leaned in closer and whispered, "So you really do know them—are you sure? There is something very off about them magically. You trust them?"

Mara nodded and started to turn away, but Brynn's hand on her arm made her focus her attention more fully on Brynn's doubts.

"Really, it's okay. They can't exactly travel under their own names, so I think that's what you're picking up on. But I know them well enough to, um, know them."

Was that a blush coloring Mara's cheeks? Brynn had only ever seen Mara do that on a few occasions. Once when the bakery girl who Mara obviously had a crush on had made an inadvertent innuendo with the word "moist," and once when Brynn had brushed some jacaranda petals out of Mara's hair.

"Are you sure you do not want me to remove the spells on them, in case they are deceiving you somehow?"

But Mara shook her head. "No, thank you. I've got this and we don't want to make things harder for them. Just—I'll see you tomorrow, okay?"

Cally and Starling came to see what was taking Mara so long and Brynn asked, "Where are you staying?"

They exchanged a look and Cally said, "Well, I guess Mrs. Dibbs would have a place for us maybe? Mara has mentioned she takes in strays."

"That's where I live," Brynn said, glad she could keep an eye on them. "You can walk with me—"

"No way," Mara interrupted. "You guys are coming home with me."

Brynn seemed to be doing a lot of frowning before speaking. "Are you sure there is room? You have a lot of strays coming and going there too." Why did these two get an immediate invitation to stay with Mara when Brynn had not yet gotten one?

Mara grinned. "Ah, but there are advantages to running the place. I have the biggest room, plus there's an extra bed from when Riley used to sleep in there, before she got her own room."

Cally grinned brightly. "So it's all set then? We're coming with you? I can't wait to meet Riley and the others."

"Has that pooka learned any manners?" Starling asked.

"You'll have to see for yourself—but Brynn did stop his singing toaster curse. Oh, and Aurora makes these vegetarian tamales that are the bomb, you've gotta try them." Mara continued chattering as the three of them walked away.

Brynn called, "Until tomorrow then, Mara," but only got a distracted wave in return.

Her stomach growling with more ire than hunger, Brynn eyed the food stalls to see what she wanted to eat tonight. Something to eat on her own, unless she was feeling lonely enough—or spiteful enough—to bring a companion home. But her heart was not really in it, bruised as it was.

Brynn was so wrapped up in unwrapping her own emotions as she came home that she belatedly realized her front door lay ajar, with the sound of pacing footsteps behind it. Brynn gripped the baguette from her shopping bag and raised it over her head like a club as she rushed inside.

Her brother whirled at her spontaneous battle cry, and casually waved a hand in Brynn's direction, freezing her in place. She glared at Brecon as she canceled the spell; he knew she could neutralize his magic, but persisted in magicking her to remind her of her own shortcomings in spellcasting.

"Brother. What are you doing here?" Brynn asked as she brushed past him and set her bag of groceries down.

He sighed, an aggravated sound she was all too familiar with. "I have come to take you home. You will marry Phoenix and he can decide how to handle you, since you will no longer be our family's problem."

"I thought I was no longer our family's problem after I left them in the restaurant?"

Brecon stopped rifling through her groceries to stare at her with narrowed eyes. Brynn had not spoken to him with such cheek since they were small, when he was still in awe of his older sister.

"Something has changed in you," he accused. "Our parents will not like it."

"I happen to like the changes and thankfully I am no longer our parents' concern."

He smiled grimly. "That is where you are wrong. Mother and Father might have been willing to pretend you never existed at all, but your loving fiancé has taken out his wrath on us. He has driven away all of our allies and friends at Court, cutting off any chance for us to better our position there.

"Father has retreated to his mountain in despair and is on his way to dwindling. Mother insists you return and fulfill your marriage contract immediately."

"No thank you." Brynn's smile was sweet and brittle as rock candy. "I am glad to hear you all have realized I indeed have value, but a life following Phoenix's orders rather than our parents' no longer appeals to me. You may relay that message to Mother."

He was silent, seething, for a moment before he asked softly, "And what do you have here that is better? As Phoenix's wife, you will be part of a second powerful family and can use that connection at Court."

"Do you not mean that you can use that connection? Your ambitions have always been more Courtly than mine."

Her brother made a sour face, so Brynn left any more flippant answers unsaid and spoke the truth. "Fine. You must remember that at home, my carreg powers mean I am punished, beaten, hidden away like a secret sin. But here, those same powers help others. I am building a life that I want, with no interference from our parents. And my new friends—loved ones—only praise me for it, sharing in my joy and satisfaction."

Brecon sneered. "And yet I find you alone in this dingy box. Where are these friends? Why are you preparing your sad little plate of food to eat by yourself?"

At his words, Brynn paused in scraping her salad from its container onto a plate. The limp greens, accompanied by a pale piece of chicken and a slice of baguette, did indeed look tragic. And yes, Mara was off with other friends instead of joining Brynn like they had planned. But that was only a temporary situation, right?

"Did you even miss me, Sister?" Brecon wheedled. "I can understand your issues with Mother and Father, but you used to think I was sweet."

"Yes, until you got old enough to see how they treated me and you adopted their contempt and meanness."

"Not all the time."

Brynn sighed and started making another plate. "Fine, you can stay long enough to take a meal with me. But then you are leaving with only a message—I am staying here."

Brecon left reluctantly, and resentfully, after dinner, full of warnings of how Brynn would regret her decision. But for all the strength she showed while he was there, doubts crowded her once she was alone again.

His arguments rang in her ears: she might love this life she was building, but what did her future look like? Would helping others with their curses or botched spells be enough to satisfy Brynn for the rest of her very long life? In truth, she had not experienced much life outside her castle and this course could actually be limiting her from other opportunities. And if Mara had feelings for her, why had she not asked Brynn to join her with Cally and Starling?

12 Brynn

After a few days of moping around the food court, with only occasional visits with Mara (who always had Cally and Starling in tow), Brynn decided a visit to her mountain was in order. Perhaps some of her listlessness could be blamed on being absent from Faerie in general and from her mountain specifically. She had no fear of being waylaid by either Brecon or Phoenix, as an oread's pilgrimage to their mountain was a sacred right and duty.

Getting there was fairly simple, as all she needed to do was climb through a window on the other side of Mrs. Dibbs's building—one which opened onto Faerie. Of course carregs could not normally travel in Faerie instantaneously like other Fae, since their magic canceled that out too. But whatever quirk caused them to be born in the first place recognized even carregs needed to be able to travel to recharge and allowed them to fold time and space for that purpose. All she had to do was draw on the connection with her mountain.

It took only an instant for Brynn to travel from the dark of a Spellmeet night and to arrive in sunshine at the foot of a vast range of peaks; she took a deep breath of cooler air, scented with firs and bracken and saxifrage. After spending time in an area of California which was most often dry and golden, the bright colors of the moss and lichen on the rock almost hurt Brynn's eyes.

Since the individual mountains took on the personality of their humanoid counterparts, some sloped into gentle, green-softened curves with inviting spots to perch. Others rose sharp and icy, looming with a forbidding brow ridge of bare stone. And the chaotic mix of rock types, with no regard for natural laws of formation, would have reduced a geologist to madness.

All of the peaks here were Brynn's family members, some so ancient that their faces—at one time, literal rock faces—had eroded into indistinguishable slopes and gravel. Others could still move their eyes to follow as she passed on the way to her own mountain. Her grandmother even roused enough to slowly drag her eyebrows into a frown, with the accompanying rock-on-rock grinding sound echoing off the slopes.

Brynn's mountain had always been smaller, like a drab foothill in the shadows of her family. Its slate shoulders hunched against the elements and crumbled easily—so it was that much more of a shock when Brynn came around the edge of her uncle's mountain and spotted her own.

Bright flowers carpeted the slopes in a riot of colors and shapes, with small streams chuckling among them. Instead of barren rocks attractive only to furtive, small creatures, these meadows were alive with swaggering hares, and lizards like nimble, jeweled brooches. For even in this, the mountains reflected their partners, and Brynn's mountain showed she was letting others in. That she was part of a thriving community.

It did more to show Brynn she was now so much more alive than any self-talk could do. Contrary to her family's lessons that caring for others was a weakness, it was in fact a strength. Something to draw on when you were unsure yourself, and returning in kind to others when needed.

Brynn sighed as she laid full-length on the mossy lawn and her magic strengthened and renewed. Her carreg magic felt different, more in tune as it rose and fell, ebbed and flowed, in time with her heartbeat and the breeze blowing across the mountain. *So this is what it feels like to be whole.*

Brynn carried that sense of wholeness and peace with her back into her Spellmeet apartment, where she showered and went to the market to get coffee before her shift at Taylor's shop. Mara waved from their food court table and for once she was by herself so Brynn went to join her.

But they had barely had a chance to catch up before Cally and Starling came over with their own breakfast; as usual, Cally had far too much food on her plate for one person to eat. And yet, somehow she managed to choke it all down while simultaneously chattering all the while. Brynn had to admit it was as impressive as it was off-putting.

As Brynn got up to leave, Cally stopped licking her plate long enough to ask, "Where are you going today?"

Brynn put her empty coffee cup down, since it seemed like this was the opening of an actual conversation. Thus far, Cally had mostly talked around Brynn, so why the change? It was worth answering politely, to see if the human gave herself away. And to earn Mara's regard for being polite to her friend.

"I help out at a nearby repair shop," Brynn said. "The owner deals with human technology but some magical items always slip through, so I help deter-mine whether those are dangerous or not."

Cally's head tilted to one side, like a dog who had heard a squeak toy in the distance. "What kind of magical items? Tools, toys, or what?"

"They can be tools or toys," Brynn answered warily. "Or a combination of the two, created with purpose or by accident. May I ask why you're sud-denly interested in my whereabouts?"

"I was wondering the same thing," Starling said with narrowed eyes.

Cally leaned over to whisper a reply, but it was easily overheard since she was an unsubtle whis-perer. "Look, it's been fun hanging out with Mara but we're not going to find what we're looking for just by going back and forth from the market to Ma-ra's house. We need to go further afield—and think about it, if someone is creating items that blend technology and magic, maybe we want to find out more about them?"

"Brynn didn't actually say that," Starling whis-pered back.

Cally nodded and turned back to Brynn. "Are any of these—do any of them have magic and tech-nology in the same thing? Like, working together?"

"Yes, but not very many work together successfully. It depends on if it is wild magic or other magic."

Cally went very still, which Brynn would not have believed was possible. That was indeed a giveaway and Brynn's senses sharpened.

"You've seen wild magic mixing with technology?" Cally asked.

"On occasion. It appears it is possible, but wild magic does not like to stay contained to an object, repeating the same action over and over. It is too capricious."

Starling stifled a laugh. "You do know what capricious means, right Cally? Unstable, volatile, temperamental—"

"Fickle, inconstant," Cally interrupted with a grumble. "Hey, I studied for the SAT even if I didn't take it. You shut up."

"Oh, burn." Starling acted like he was shaking off sparks, and he and Mara laughed while Cally glowered.

But why would Cally act like describing wild magic as "capricious" was a personal affront? Did it have something to do with the oddness which Brynn kept sensing around her and Starling? There was an obvious way to find out.

"Would you like to come along and see for yourself, Cally?" Brynn asked. "I am sure Taylor would not mind an extra pair of hands, though you would have to negotiate any pay with them."

Cally sprang up from the table. "Yes, I would like to come with you. Starling can go 'entertain' himself."

Her tone of voice said that was a euphemism, but Brynn was listening for the grating on her carreg nerves which happened sometimes when Cally spoke Starling's or Mara's names. Or on occasion when Cally spoke her own name, for that matter. It had not happened this time, however, so Brynn waited while Cally gathered her things. Which apparently included bagging up the rest of Mara's breakfast to take with her in case Cally got hungry later.

They walked in silence for a moment before the human girl's chatter started up again. "Thanks for inviting me. Mara doesn't want me staying home with Riley—can you believe she thinks we're bad influences on each other?—so I've been going everywhere with her instead. But she shoots me one of her death glances if I try to talk to her customers. It's like when I was trapped in that dungeon—"

She stumbled as she missed her footing. "I mean, like getting trapped in a dungeon. The kind of imaginary dungeon that people get trapped in and they aren't allowed to talk to anyone. I'm sure you've heard of those, right?"

Brynn agreed with Mara that Riley and Cally were much alike; they both spoke as if they were trying to get all their words out at once, instead of spacing breaths among the run-on sentences. Brynn decided to treat Cally like Riley by ignoring her conversational asides, and hopefully they could better communicate.

"I know what you mean. Growing up in my family's castle was just such an experience as your imaginary dungeon."

Cally gasped and asked, "You grew up in a dungeon? What did you do?"

Did this human really agree that punishing a child with imprisonment was reasonable? Brynn's voice went cold as she answered, "I was born a carreg, and that was enough to make my parents punish me."

Cally turned red again. "Sorry, I didn't mean like 'what did you do to deserve that?' because of course that would be messed up. I meant, how did you survive? How did you get out?"

"Mara helped me see a way out of my family's toxic patterns." Brynn appreciated how well those human terms fit; most Fae would consider her parents' cruel treatment justified. Even conservative, in some circles. "Once I was further away from their voices, I could stop listening. And tune into my powers instead."

Cally made a face. "Yeah, those toxic voices can be tough. But Mara's good at helping that way, right? She just accepts whatever weirdness you throw her way."

"Yes, I am very grateful she is in my life."

Cally laughed. "And once she's in your life, you won't get her out. She's a bulldog."

Jealousy flared up so hot that Brynn was not able to speak, until she tamped it down and casually asked, "You speak from experience, I can tell. How long have you been friends?"

"We went to school together, back in the before time. We had a few classes together but we weren't exactly friends—until she decided to make me one of her projects. And she was okay with meeting Starling and before I knew it, we were all best buds. She gets me."

"Yes, she seems to be able to bond with many types of people. But hold a moment—did she know Starling was Fae when she met him in that 'before time'?"

Cally started to answer, but stopped. Her face showed a series of conflicting emotions—hesitancy, worry, fear, and calculation—before she got a hold of herself. At this crack in her guise, Brynn readied herself to push harder, but the human girl spoke.

"Yes, she did know him. Since he's a corbin, Starling worked out trades with Mara so he could come visit me in her body. By the time the Shifting happened, she had already been exposed to the Fae—" Cally interrupted herself to snort with laughter at her own choice of words,"—so she didn't have much trouble adjusting when everything got put through the blender. She's one of a handful of people I've kept in touch with from before the Border went away. We haven't seen each other as much as I'd like but we picked up right where we left off, it's amazing."

"She's amazing," they both said at the same time, and the shared opinion helped Brynn relax her prickly attitude.

They walked a few more steps in a comfortable silence until Cally asked, "Why haven't you been spending much time with Mara since we got here? She talks about you all the time and said she misses you."

Brynn was genuinely taken aback. "She does? It seemed like she wanted to spend time with you and Starling so I was letting her have her space. Plus, I was not invited to join in with...however it is you spend your time."

Brynn's hurt must have shown in her voice, so she stopped walking when Cally's reaction was to chuckle. Cally caught her wounded expression and hastily spoke up.

"I'm sorry, I wasn't laughing at you. Well, maybe a little, because you made it sound like we're spending our time in non-stop threesomes."

"Are you not?" Brynn asked with a raised eyebrow. "I would, if—" She stopped short at saying aloud that she would if Mara was one of the three.

"Well, I guess I don't need to have the 'what are your intentions towards my friend' talk with you. It's obvious you're smitten with her, and so is she. Smitten with you, I mean, not with herself."

How was this something Cally knew before Brynn herself did? "Mara is smitten with me? She has told you this?"

"No, not in as many words," Cally admitted. "It's just that I've never seen her like she is when she talks about you. Like you're simultaneously the most endearing and the most terrifying cuddly animal. Like a polar bear or a raccoon or something."

Brynn wished Cally did not speak in such a roundabout way. "You are saying she wants me to scare her while she cuddles me?"

"No, no, she wants you to—listen, has she told you about any of her past relationships?"

"In passing. I get the sense there are more than she has mentioned."

"Yeah, she's young and uninhibited and pan so she hooked up with a lot of Fae at first. But she got hurt a few times—I think she thought it would be like a poly relationship among humans, but it wasn't. I don't know if you can even call it a relationship when most Fae don't consider humans too far above animals...but you know what? You should probably have a conversation with her about this. I'd probably confuse the issue and she's a better source of info on how she feels. So, talk to her."

Cally had indeed confused Brynn, but her tone seemed to be reassuring. That encouragement might be the push Brynn needed to overcome her fear of ruining her current relationship with Mara. Having the "what are your intentions" conversation, as Cally put it, in the hope Mara's intentions were just as naughty.

They reached Taylor's shop and Cally disappeared down an aisle with a whoop, leaving Brynn shaking her head in exasperation. She had not even had time to warn the girl against touching things if she did not know what they were.

Riley had learned the difficult way when the pair of binoculars she picked up caused her to sprout eyes randomly on her body before Brynn cancelled the spell. Let Cally learn the same way, Brynn decided with a shrug.

Brynn made her way to the table that had been set aside for her, and found a pile of objects already waiting. These were the things people dropped off for her to fix, the things they regretted buying or when they had second thoughts about that custom spell they had added. The spellcaster may have had malicious intentions or had been just proficient enough to think they knew what they were doing (when it was obvious by the results they did not). The result was the same: they needed a no-frills removal of the spell, an easy enough task for a carreg.

She worked her way through a kazoo that repeated a song on a loop *ad nauseam* (it was currently humming that song humans pranked each other with), a bottomless cauldron which only served tofu chili, and other small annoyances. Then it was time to patrol the aisles for magical items that had slipped in, and it would give Brynn a chance to track down Cally, whose silence made Brynn nervous.

13 Avery

I'd always loved thrifting, and Taylor's shop was like a thrift store and junkyard had mated, or maybe they'd taken turns throwing up. For someone with my attention span, it meant picking one thing up and marveling at it for about two seconds before something else caught my eye. And that was only the stuff at my eye level; the roof of this old metal barn soared high above, with layers of arcane objects hanging from the rafters.

Walking backwards with my gaze turned upwards, I saw the frame of a motorcycle, with something like desiccated pumpkins in place of the wheels. *Who thought that up? Some crazy person out for a gourd time?* I snorted to myself and made a mental note to share the pun with Lonan later. He would tease me about it being so lame, but at least he'd humor me with a laugh.

I found a bunch of animated toys who had built themselves a town in a steamer trunk, creating a civilization in about six square feet. Everything was there: a park with bonsai forest, a seedy corner of cigar-box bars, and even a chapel made from a glass terrarium.

But apparently they didn't like being watched, because a couple of action figures and toy soldiers teamed up to shoot pop beads at me, using a sling-shot like a catapult. I dodged the rain of plastic pro-jectiles and screamed, "I am your God, do not renounce me!" as I ducked into the next aisle.

That's when I saw them: a skin-and-bone pair of wings, if the skin was pleather and the bones were PVC pipe, hanging from wires anchored in the raft-ers. The important part was they were sized for a human, and maybe they were magicked for flying.

If I climbed on top of that rack of old radios I might be able to reach them. The sound of falling objects as I scrambled up attracted the shop's own-er, who Brynn had already told me was an enby named Taylor.

They watched me for a moment and said, "I hope you brought enough money to cover breaking all those things you've knocked down. You could, you know, tell me what you're after and ask for help?"

I panted as I reached the top of the collection and asked, "These wings—do they work?"

"Sort of. I've been meaning to get Brynn to take a look at them. You may as well bring them down."

I think Taylor meant I should carry the wings down, but once I freed them from the wires they quivered in my hands. An obvious pair of shoulder straps curled around my arms, not quite hitting me right until I helpfully turned my back to the setup. Then they wrapped around my shoulders, and a couple of times around my torso, until they hugged me like a sports bra.

"Wait!" Taylor called. "You do not want to do that—those wings are not reliable."

But my feet were already hovering a few inches from the top of the shelves as the flapping grew stronger and settled into a rhythm.

"Oh no," I said, my words sounding unconvincing to even my own ears. I hadn't flown in a long time and I missed my wings, a gift from the wyvern part of my family tree. They had gone away with my wild magic, just when I was getting good at flying. *Let's see how much I remember.*

Taylor ducked as I swept low over their head, and then I swooped up to the ceiling in a graceful arc. Even though the ceilings were high, it didn't give me enough space and I looped to the open barn doors. I passed Brynn's startled face as the wings carried me into the sunlight and the yard outside.

A yelp shot out of me as the wings picked up speed and tried to lift me higher. It might have worked on somebody who had no flying experience, but I remembered how to shift my weight and balance to control my flight path. The wings and I struggled for control: every time they drove me into a dive or a steep climb, I turned it into my own curving arc above Taylor's piles of outdoor junk.

Finally, I detected a sulkiness in the wings' beats, and they let me swing back to the shop doors, where Brynn and Taylor waited. The shop owner applauded but Brynn frowned like a disapproving nun.

Taylor called, "Impressive! It looks like you were born to flying! But you should know those wings are glitchy—they give out without any notice."

"That's why the previous owners sold them to you?"

"None of the previous owners survived."

I chewed my lip as that sank in, but so far the wings and I had found a truceful tempo. We worked in harmony to hover, a move I was never able to do with my natural wings.

Brynn said, "If anything happens to you, Mara will have my head. Try to fly lower so I may cancel the spell on them."

Apprehension shuddered through the wings and they whipped me away. "I don't think they like that idea!" I shouted.

Now it was a real battle between the wings trying to whisk me to the horizon and me trying every trick I knew to throw my weight around and throw the wings off their path. Far below, Brynn and Taylor were mere specks standing next to a barn the size of a Monopoly hotel.

"Can we come to some sort of agreement?" I asked the wings. "I won't let Brynn cancel your spell, and I'd like it if we could go flying together again soon. Wouldn't you rather get out in the fresh air instead of hanging out in a dark barn all the time?"

At first I thought the wings weren't listening—or maybe they weren't somewhat sentient like I'd thought—but then I felt myself level out. With a whispered thanks, I guided the wings into a spiral which would eventually take us to the ground.

I waved to let Brynn and Taylor know everything was okay, and even added a few fancy figure eights to my spiral. Right in the middle of a loop, I was laughing when I felt the wings shudder again.

They did a few stuttering, desperate flaps and then wrapped around me as we started to plummet. I didn't even have enough breath to scream as the wings flapped like a loose tarp in the rush of wind—acting like a costume piece made from pleather and PVC again.

Taylor's yard approached way too fast as my brain went into overdrive and tried to think up some way out of this. *Could I go into a skydiver position and slow my fall? Nope, probably not high enough up when the freefall started. Should I go limp? Roll up into a ball? Just enjoy the show of my life passing in front of my eyes?*

Below, Taylor threw a couple of pillows onto the ground and Brynn gestured like I should aim for them. *Yeah, right, a few pillows will make all the difference.* I opened my mouth to yell that I had no control, but the rushing air stole my words. And I kept plummeting.

I squeezed my eyes shut, so I wouldn't know the exact moment of impact, when suddenly I was yanked from behind. Worse pressure on my body even than when I went bungee jumping and I had thought the harness was going to slice through me as I hit the end of the cord.

I couldn't see through a haze of pain and breathlessness, until the pressure lessened enough for me

take in a harsh, gasping breath. A coughing fit followed it, and I really wished it hadn't because it felt
like every single rib had been crunched like an ice
cream cone in a troll's fist.

But then I heard urgent voices nearby and saw
the top of Brynn's and Taylor's heads as the wings
floated me down like a dandelion seed. My feet
touched the pillows and hands guided me gently to
lay prone. I made a horrible wheezing sound that no
person should make as I tried to breathe; dark tun-
nel walls started to narrow my vision and everything went black.

"Can you hear me?" someone asked.

I stretched luxuriously before mumbling, "Yeah,
can't I sleep a little longer?"

"No, you may not! You need to tell us what happened."

I opened my eyes and saw Brynn leaning over
me, her face filled with fear, or anger, or maybe a
combination. I opened my mouth to say, "Uh, I fell,
what do you mean what happened?" but then more
details came back to me. Falling, and the impossi-
bleness of me not falling at the end. *Had the wings
come to life, like actual life?*

"The wings saved me, right? I'll have to thank
them."

Taylor shook their head. "They flew away on their own. They're—alive, somehow."

So I hadn't imagined the part where they Pinnochioed. I tried to sit up but Taylor held me down, rearranging a magic bone-knitting patch so it stayed in contact with my torso.

I grumped, "When I checked them over, they were just...junk put together. Even if they did have a built-in murder setting."

Brynn nodded, saying, "The spell on them worked exactly as it was supposed to. It was meant to lure a foolish human into flying, and then to drop them to their death. The wings had done it before and would do it again, as the curse dictated."

"But they didn't kill me! I mean, the wings may have a sick sense of humor, but they ultimately caught me before I splatted."

Brynn asked Taylor to get me some water and waited for them to go inside the shop before she said, "It wasn't the wings that caught you. That was another magic, but I have no explanation for why it helped you. Do you know of some reason why wild magic would go out of its way to save you, Cally?"

My breath stuttered and Brynn leaned forward, reaching a hand to me. I covered my reaction with a cough until I was calm enough to ask, "Wild magic, huh? Are you sure that's what it was?"

"I know wild magic when I hear it," she said sharply. "Do you claim to know nothing about it?"

"How could I? I was unconscious. And everyone knows wild magic is unpredictable." I sat up gingerly as Taylor approached with a glass of water.

Brynn stared at me while I drank. Or more like, she listened at me, with her eyes unfocused and her head cocked to the side. *Well, a second ago she did say she* hears *wild magic.*

I asked, "Is there wild magic here right now?"

"No, merely the residue," she answered. "But why are you lying to me?"

"I'm not." And my words had the ring of truth to them because I hadn't lied; I had just talked around the question. A ploy I'd learned from that tricksy corbin, Lonan.

Brynn and Taylor exchanged a look like neither of them believed me before the shopkeeper spoke. "The wild magic Brynn is talking about, it didn't only save you from falling. It changed the wings into living tissue, with something like a jellyfish or octopus making up the harness. The creature let me take you out of its grasp and then it flew away. I think it even winked at me!"

Brynn confirmed Taylor's story with a nod. "It is true that once the wild magic transformed the wings, nothing I tried with my carreg magic made a difference. The essence had been changed, of course, not merely the appearance."

"That's weird," I said, and I didn't even have to fake my puzzlement. I had been trying to reconnect with wild magic ever since we'd separated and had no real response. Sure, sometimes it affected things around me and it had even pranked me once or twice, but it was too skittish to stick around long. Too capricious.

"Is that all you have to say about it?" Taylor asked.

I nodded wearily. Not so much body-weary (because I felt great now thanks to Taylor using the medi-patch), but tired of lying. *It might be best to bring Brynn in on the secrets before she does something hasty out of ignorance.*

"Let's go back and catch up *with* Lonan and Missa," I said, and then winced as I realized I'd used their real names. But the wild magic must not have affected the spell that covered my misspoken words because Taylor didn't react. Did Brynn's sour expression mean she'd heard something was off though? Who could tell anymore? I wasn't exactly famous for correctly interpreting social cues.

Whatever Brynn's feelings, she helped me up. I didn't really need it, but also didn't want to rub it in her face that I was fine since she seemed to be suspicious about how I'd been saved. *Hell, I'd like to know how, too.* After thanking Taylor for their help, we left them to their now-quiet shop and Brynn and I headed back to the marketplace.

We walked in silence until Brynn blurted, "You may not owe Taylor an explanation, but you owe them for a very valuable healing spell. They had a buyer for it—a lucrative sale, I might add—but they used it on your injuries instead. Else, you would not have survived. If you were being cagey because you did not want to reveal secrets in front of Taylor, now is your chance to explain in confidence."

She sounded completely fed up with me but I didn't want to lie or stretch the truth again, so I shook my head. Brynn deserved more since she'd tried to help me, but they weren't only my secrets. Lonan and Missa had their own reasons for laying low—mostly to do with being associated with Avery Flynn and the destruction of the Border—and I wasn't going to out them without their permission. Missa/Mara had even changed her name so no one would link us together.

I hadn't been listening as Brynn had continued to speak, but a word caught my attention. "What did you just say?" I asked.

"Wyverns. I said I had the opportunity to social-ize with wyverns over the last year and I know what their wings look like up close. Would you care to comment on why the wild magic chose to model the new wing/tentacle creature on wyvern appendages? It could have chosen anything."

I sighed; obviously Brynn wasn't going to let this go. "Look, Brynn, I know you want some answers. Let me talk to—to Mara and Starling and then I'll see how much I can share with you. Deal? We're almost to the food court so you shouldn't have to wait too much longer."

Still, she persisted. "If Phoenix sent you here, I need to know—"

I walked faster, cutting off her words. I ignored anything she said after that, only asking her to give me a minute with our friends. She wasn't happy, but she hung back as I took Missa and Lonan aside.

"Hey guys," I said in a low voice. "Something happened and we may need to let Brynn in on a few things. Apparently wild magic was involved, and if she knows about magic like she says maybe she can help us."

We all turned to look at Brynn, who was pacing and mumbling to herself in increasing agitation.

"How much do you trust her?" Lonan asked Missa.

"I mean, I trust her a lot—but this is big. Too big for us to entirely control, once she knows."

"So you don't think it's a good idea to tell her who we are?" I asked. "Even if it helps us get closer to maybe figuring out what wild magic has been doing with itself all this time?"

"I don't know!" Missa's words wrenched out of her. "Maybe I can talk to her and ask to give us some more time to think about it."

I opened my mouth to respond, but then it felt like someone splashed me with cold water. I gasped, blinking, and felt something weird on my face. I reached up to pull it off—*omygawd it's the fake face*—just as Missa shoved me under the table we were standing near. Lonan's "face" dropped to the ground next to me as Missa made some inarticulate, panicked noises.

Then Brynn was there, triumphant. "I knew these two were hiding their true selves somehow! Now you can see it too, Mara, and—"

"What have you done??" Mara's horrified question cut off Brynn's rant.

Brynn gaped uncertainly while Lonan and Missa exchanged looks. The people nearest to us had noticed something was going on and their voices raised as they pointed our way.

Lonan's head dropped for a moment before he climbed onto a table and said, "Yes, it is I, the

Butcher Bird! I am ready to take up the mantle of my Aunt Maeve, Queen of Faerie."

Gasps met his announcement, but his distraction worked as he continued to walk across the tabletops and lead everyone away from my hiding spot. Everyone except Missa and Brynn.

14 Brynn

What have you done?? Mara's words echoed in Brynn's ears, and she was no longer so certain it was wise to remove the spells from Mara's friends.

"I am sorry if I have done something wrong," she whispered to Mara. "I knew a spell was hiding their true selves from view and when I saw wyvern traits around Cally I was afraid Phoenix had sent them to harm me or you—"

"Shut. Up," Mara gritted, and grabbed Brynn's arm painfully to emphasize her words. "Do not talk about those things here."

Brynn gasped but did not try to break free; she was too shocked by Mara's behavior. Never had she seen the human like this: icy with rage and horror, like Brynn's own mother often was. It made Brynn reflexively cower, as she had in those situations.

"Mara, please, I can fix this somehow if you will let me..." Brynn trailed off into a wordless whine and furtively tried to free her arm from Mara's grip.

Mara seemed to come to herself then and dropped her hands to her sides. "You have no idea what you've done, so how can you fix it? This is some serious shit. Why didn't you trust me? Because I'm a human and you decided I needed saving?"

Brynn only hung her head, shame and the impulse to flee warring against her promise to fix things.

Mara stepped closer and Brynn flinched, but her friend only said in a low voice, "If you really want to make up for this, take her away from here. Don't let anyone see either of you, and hide her someplace safe. Are you able to do that? Can I trust you with this?"

Brynn nodded and Mara squeezed her hand before she waded into the crowd. Brynn almost ran after her, to ask if Mara would ever forgive her, but she did not have the luxury to follow her heart (and insecurities). Not if she was going to earn forgiveness.

Mara's cries of "Is that really Lonan the corbin there, come to claim his crown?" drew the rest of the stragglers in her wake. She led them away from where Cally still huddled in the shadow beneath the table. Brynn knelt and met Cally's eyes—except that if Starling was actually the notorious Lonan in disguise, who was Cally really? *Could it be..?*

Brynn rocked back on her heels, staring harder at the human. With a sigh, Cally/Avery Flynn nodded and asked, "How do we get out of here?"

Brynn glanced around and saw most of the booths in the marketplace had been abandoned. She darted over to one selling clothing and grabbed a hooded cloak from a hanger. Throwing some money onto the chair inside the booth, Brynn came back and handed it to Avery.

Avery looked at it and said, "You want me to walk out of here in a cloak and hope that's inconspicuous?"

"Do you have another idea? Lonan and Mara will not hold everyone's attention forever, you know."

Shaking her head, Avery donned the cloak and slipped out from beneath the table.

"Hunch your shoulders to change your silhouette," Brynn advised. "If you can make it to Mara's vehicle, we can flee faster."

"Suddenly you're an expert on running away, but it didn't occur to you there was a good reason we were in disguise?" Avery muttered, but followed Brynn's suggestion and doubled over like she had a stomachache.

It seemed like Lonan's ploy to attract attention was working because they did not encounter anyone until they reached Mara's rickshaw and started to climb aboard. The man who ran the ice cream stand near where she always parked it emerged and glared at them.

"Hey, Mara didn't say anything to me about someone borrowing her rickshaw," he said with arms folded.

"Oh, we are her friends," Brynn answered while Avery huddled further into her cloak. "We are not stealing it."

He scoffed. "Mara has a lot of friends but she always remembers to tell me if she's lending this out. I think you'd better leave her ride here until she tells me otherwise."

Avery started groaning in the back of the vehicle, making such horrible noises that even Brynn did a double take.

"Please, Mister, she's taking me to the doctor," Avery said. "I've got some horrible stomach thing."

But the man was still not convinced. "Oh yeah? Let me look at you."

"No!" Avery and Brynn blurted together.

"It is contagious to humans," Brynn explained. "That's why I am taking our friend instead of Mara."

He still seemed hesitant and Brynn was glad this man was so conscientious, but they had already lost too much time. She settled into the seat and pedals, planning to just ride away.

But the man reached for the handlebars—until a gush of something orange and chunky projected from Avery and nearly hit him. He dodged backwards and they were able to make their getaway.

"Hey, these are peaches from a snack cup!" His voice called after them but they kept going.

"Lonan makes fun of me for always having food squirreled away in my pockets, but it comes in handy sometimes."

Brynn grunted in response as she put all her effort into pedaling as fast as she was able. Once she fell into a rhythm, she was able to concentrate on the next challenge: where should they go? The old quarry outside of Spellmeet perhaps? Somewhere in Faerie?

Avery must have been wondering also because she volunteered, "We can't go to Mara's. If they figure out she's Avery Flynn's friend Missa, they will look for me there.

"Oh, hey, I can say our real names now without them morphing into the fake names. Your spell must have fried that magic too."

"I do not cast spells, I remove them," Brynn puffed in answer. "But no mind—I might be able to hide you on my mountain in Faerie."

"So many alarms would go off if I even stuck the tip of my nose in Faerie that I would be captured for sure. Where else did you have in mind?"

"I am afraid I do not know many other places. Taylor's workshop perhaps? It does have a lot of boltholes among the chaos but it also has frequent customers. There is an old quarry on the outskirts of town—"

"Nah," Avery interrupted. "Some rock trolls have taken that over. They would squish me to death first and ask questions later."

"Oh, are they necromancers as well?" Brynn half turned in her seat, letting the pedals coast. "Because then we could kill you and let everyone see your corpse, and then these necromancer trolls could bring you back to life when no one is looking for you any longer."

Avery's eyes went wide. "Oh, um, as charming as that sounds, it was only a figure of speech when I said they ask questions later. As far as I know, they're regular, people-squishing rock trolls."

"Hmm." Brynn started pedaling again. "Then I am afraid my apartment is the only place I can think of. It is not terribly defensible, but if we needed to escape into Faerie and reach my mountain, all we need to do is flee through a window on the other side of the building."

"I don't know...do you have good wifi? Any video games?"

Brynn glanced over her shoulder and said, "I do not believe those are priorities right now—"

"Kidding! I suppose your apartment has an advantage in that no one knows of a connection between the notorious Avery Flynn and Lady Brynn. It will have to do until we find anything better."

Brynn turned down an alley and took a circuitous route to Mrs. Dibbs's building, not even bothering to hide the rickshaw once they arrived since it was parked outside so frequently. When Brynn and Avery were halfway up the stairs, Mrs. Dibbs's door opened and she called after Brynn but they hustled to the apartment without replying.

They each breathed a sigh of relief when they were safely shut in Brynn's apartment. Avery discarded the cloak and paced around the living room.

"I hope Lonan is okay," she said. "He told me he would give himself up if it seemed like we were discovered, but I asked him not to. You can't really tell corbins what to do though."

"No, you cannot."

Avery stopped pacing and stared at Brynn. "You can't tell carregs what to do either, apparently. Didn't Missa—your Mara—tell you to leave it alone when you asked about why we were hiding something?"

Brynn winced. "Yes, she did. And I was willing to, until the wild magic saved you and made me suspicious if you had connections to Phoenix or other wyverns."

Avery turned to her with a teeth-baring smile. "Like my wyvern traits that make me want to tear you limb from limb for threatening my friends' safety?"

Brynn stumbled back a few steps, turning pale. If keeping hidden was the only thing stopping Avery Flynn from using her full magic, what would she do now that she was exposed?

"I—I did not threaten anyone. I did not even know Mara was your friend, or that Starling was Lonan. But I *am* sorry I was the instrument for undoing your disguises."

When Avery made no reply, Brynn stammered, "C-can you make new masks?"

"Not without a lot of trouble, and we'd probably have to actually do the dark magic this time around." Avery noticed how Brynn had put the kitchen counter between them and added, "I was joking about tearing you limb from limb. Mostly. For now, anyway."

Brynn did not find that as comforting as perhaps Avery meant it to be. She thought it safer to direct the conversation to something less violent. "Would you like a cup of tea? And perhaps a peanut butter and jelly sandwich?"

Avery perked up. "What kind of jelly?"

"I have grape jelly and strawberry jam on hand."

"Have you ever mixed them?"

"Two flavors on one sandwich? That sounds decadent." Brynn relaxed a little as Avery rubbed her hands together gleefully. Brynn wondered if she should have clued in to Avery's wyvern nature from her appetite alone, which was even more insatiable than Riley's—who was a growing child.

Together, Brynn and Avery formed an assembly line for their snacks and then sat at the table. Brynn was grateful the sticky peanut butter kept them from talking for a bit, as she had no idea what to say to Avery Flynn.

But after devouring four sandwiches, Avery's teasing was back. "No offense, but your apartment doesn't have any touches of Brynn-ness at all. How come you haven't made yourself at home here?"

Brynn looked around, seeing her residence through new eyes. The only decor items were gifts Mara had given her, plus a series of crayon drawings from Riley stuck on the refrigerator. The scuffed walls and worn furnishings were otherwise a blank canvas, but it soothed her after a day's work and overstimulation.

Brynn explained, "This place was one of the empty units after the couple who lived here disappeared; we kept the pieces that we were able to clean the bloodstains off of and stored everything else. The splatter was surprisingly spread out, so there was not much to save."

Brynn would have said more, but as she had spoken she noticed Avery's teasing grin had gradually fossilized. Now it was stretched in place, and something about Avery's frozen expression made her own heart beat a little faster with anxiety. *Why did it look familiar?*

Brynn realized all in an instant that she was recognizing the expression from her own mirror—it was what she looked like after spending time with her family. The brittle smile that somehow held up under the onslaught of barbs and contempt until it melted under the flood of tears in the privacy of her room. Was Avery herself still wearing a mask, and actually falling apart under the façade of a jester?

She reached out to take Avery's hand and the human reflexively tried to pull away. Brynn kept a hold of it, not tight enough to cause further panic but tight enough to make Avery look at her. What passed between them then was a mutual acknowledgement, that each knew what it was like to live with guilt, pain, and grief. And to try to keep moving forward until those things could be replaced with happier feelings.

Avery smiled, and this time it was genuine. She gave Brynn's hand a squeeze and let go. "Okay, now that my identity is out of the bag, let's talk about the wild magic you sensed at Taylor's shop? Did it seem like—did the wild magic recognize me, do you think? Was it already near me or did it get called or something when I fell?"

"My carreg magic does not usually show me details like that."

As an example of how her magic worked, Brynn told her how she had unraveled the curse on Mrs. Dibbs's house. Avery let her get to the part where Brynn had sensed two distinct wild magic signatures before she interrupted.

"What were they like, the two wild magics? Others have told me they don't get a clear sense of wild magic, just that it leaves a distinctive residue that something is off. Almost how the Sight works for me when I first notice a break in the pattern."

"That is where my carreg abilities do have an advantage. I hear spells and magic as distinct tunes, and the type of music imparts clues on the nature of it. So two wild magics will sound like individuals to me, as different as a bassoon is from a tin whistle."

"Kind of like synesthesia? The wild magics really sound like music to you?" Avery asked, with longing in her voice.

"Yes, those were specific examples." Brynn watched Avery closely for a moment, as the human girl's eyes went unfocused and sad. "It is unusual to find wild magic unattached to someone, is it not? From what I learned in our Fae history books, wild magic is anchored to one person much like how the royal magic attaches itself to the true ruler of Faerie. Thus, imprisoning Merlin also caged his wild magic. And yet, as soon as I started using my magic in Spellmeet I came across two free-roaming wild magics. Is there perhaps more to wild magic and its role in the destruction of the border than I have been told?"

Avery grimaced. "Not for lack of trying. Lonan and I did what we could to spread the truth of Merlin's plans, but we didn't have much time before we were forced into hiding. And while we concentrated on not being ripped apart by an angry mob, the story got rewritten by the Fae and humans who made it through the Shifting. That's the version everyone knows, pieced together from experiences but no insights into the actual facts."

Was this the source of Avery's anguish? Being blamed for the worst thing to happen to either world?

"I will listen to your story," Brynn said.

After they brewed a fresh pot of tea, Avery launched into the simplified—yet still incredibly convoluted—story of how Merlin wanted to finally die and tried to take every living thing with him. Avery had protected as much as she could by pulling people, Fae, places, and things from Faerie and the human world into a protected pocket of time and space, essentially.

"I should have gotten a Nobel prize for proving and disproving theories of quantum physics, instead of getting a price on my head," Avery concluded with a sigh. "I'd settle for not being blamed for all the things Merlin did, but since his wild magic isn't anchored to him anymore it can't be traced back to him."

"Merlin's wild magic is the bassoon?" Brynn guessed. "But you are still alive and your wild magic—the tin whistle—is also running amok. Did you give it up willingly?"

"Yes and no. He tricked me into allowing him access to my magic, claiming that our magics could work better together to solve the problem of the border disintegrating. He kinda failed to mention I would no longer have any access to my own powers—and that his solution was utterly final. I was able to get my wild magic back for a short while, but the time it spent under his control damaged the connection. Or maybe traumatized it, I don't know. My wild magic ran off and whatever was left of Merlin's is loose too."

"You have no magic then?"

Avery shook her head. "Can't even get common spells to work."

"If you were safe in hiding, why did you and Lonan don disguises and risk exposure then?" Brynn asked.

"We did it to keep a promise to Queen Maeve."

Brynn was so startled that she leaped to her feet, knocking her chair over. "The queen is alive?"

"No, I'm sorry, I probably should have said 'the late Queen Maeve' to make it clearer. Her mountain didn't make it through the Shifting so she just..."

Avery trailed off and Brynn nodded to show she understood. There was not a single person, human or Fae, who had not lost something or someone in that Shifting. According to Avery's story, what was left—or how much was saved—was a stroke of good fortune. Brynn sat back down and they breathed together in silence, thinking of all those who were lost to this terrible thing. The queen was one of many, but the civil war tearing Brynn's homeworld apart proved how important one person could be.

15 Brynn

Avery broke the silence with a flood of inane chatter that was obviously an attempt to lighten the somber tone of their conversation. Brynn went along with it, launching into an anecdote from a few weeks before.

"I came to pick up Mara for movie night and found the ceiling in the room below Riley's dripping slime and stagnant water. The smell when Mara opened the bedroom door to investigate nearly felled us! Riley floated on her bed as if it were a lily pad, trying to appear as if there was nothing unusual happening, and too stubborn to ask for help.

"It turned out she lured some pixies into her room with a sugar water feeder, not realizing that if they decided to stay they would remake her room into a pocket of their home glade. These particular pixies came from the edge of a swamp, so.... I doubt that house will ever smell the same, Aurora's efforts with sweet-scented flowers notwithstanding."

Avery laughed until tears started. "That sounds like something I would do! Lonan has joked about Riley being my long-lost child, but of course it's not possible."

"Why not?" Brynn asked.

Avery stared at her. "Um, because the age gap is not right and I've never been pregnant?"

Brynn chuckled. "I am sorry, I am horrible at guessing the age of humans. Although if you are not strictly human, perhaps you age differently any-way?"

"Maybe if my wild magic had stayed with me I would have. But my wyvern-ness seemed to run off at the same time—ironic that I miss something so much when I didn't want it in the first place, right? I think now I'm as human as Mara or Riley. Speaking of, don't you think we should have heard something from them by now? Have you checked your voicemail?"

Brynn got up to check the answering machine but it displayed 0.

"Whoa, is that a land line?" Avery looked at the phone like it was some ancient artifact.

"Yes, cell phones do not work in this building. Although the curse has been removed, magic and technology are still unpredictable here."

"But can you make a call out? And try to reach Mara or someone at her house?"

Mara did not answer her cell phone, but Aurora did answer at the house, saying Mara had not been home yet.

"She is probably picking Riley up from potions class," Brynn told Avery after she hung up, "if she is keeping to her usual routine."

"That would be less suspicious," Avery reluctantly agreed. "I hate feeling out of the loop though."

"Perhaps I should go and find Mara?"

Mara would be on foot, since the rickshaw was here outside Mrs. Dibbs's building. She might appreciate Brynn delivering her transportation to her so they did not have to walk the entire way.

Brynn had to convince Avery that she should not come also—disguised in a raincoat—and then climbed into the rickshaw. But even allowing for tiredness, her feet did not seem to want to pedal very fast. Doubt weighed them down.

The earlier crack in Avery's veneer of cheerful mania had made Brynn think about her own family, and her attempts to build a new one. Brynn had not confessed to Avery that part of the reason she had not made her mark on her apartment was that she considered it temporary quarters—not because she wanted to leave Spellmeet, but because she hoped Mara would move in with her or invite Brynn to live in the house. Perhaps the jokes she had heard about relationships between human females progressing so quickly to moving in together were unfounded?

And now, what if Mara was so angry at Brynn for revealing her friends that she no longer wanted to see Brynn? After all, she had not known Brynn for nearly as long as Avery and Lonan and they had been through a lot together. Both emotionally and, perhaps, physically. What was one more Fae to her, really? Someone whom Mara liked well enough, but not enough to give her the benefit of the doubt if it came to mistakes? Revealing Avery and Lonan was a huge mistake.

Brynn did not have many points of reference to predict the depths of Mara's feelings; most of the times they had been alone together, Mara went out of her way to make it clear they were not on a date. It was like the idea of getting serious with Brynn terrified her, and based on the comments Avery had made earlier, perhaps that was the case. Would Mara have been so hesitant if Brynn was human rather than Fae?

Her own Fae relationship experience was no help either, since the closest she had come was an affair with a dryad. His magic could not ensnare her (a novelty) and he was a considerate lover while his attention fixed upon her, but he moved on after he grew bored. The few other Fae partners took up with her during their rebellious 200s, as a way to shock their parents.

Most Fae households included pretty, human servants for sexual release, but instead Brynn used her carreg powers to give the humans a choice by removing the glamour that let them—made them—enjoy lovemaking. Once they were alone with Brynn and aware of their surroundings, all they wanted was her help to return to their own world and families. Brynn had done what she could to help, but any servants caught fleeing were cruelly punished by Brynn's mother. As was Brynn, until it was ground into her that it was better to leave the humans to their glamoured fates. At least then they did not suffer so much.

After some futile stops without finding Mara, it seemed to make the most sense for Brynn to wait for her at the house. Brynn stopped and got enough donuts for everyone on the way and was welcomed into the chaotic household.

Finally, Riley rushed in the door like a wind sprite and Mara followed behind her. Mara stopped short when she saw Brynn waiting in the kitchen, but did not say anything. Aurora looked between them and picked up the box of donuts.

"Whoever wants donuts better come get them in the garden," Aurora called and led everyone outside.

"How is she?" Mara asked once they were alone.

"She is fine, although worried about you and Lon—"

Mara's warning hiss cut off Brynn's words, so she finished with, "Worried about both of you."

Mara sank into a chair, relieved. "He's at Court—he tried to slip away from the crowd, but some of his 'supporters' were already there by that point. They were not going to let him disappear again. I didn't have much trouble myself, not after a Fae threw some kind of spell at me to see if I was—you know who. It was obvious I wasn't her so they lost interest in me after that."

Now it was Brynn's turn to drop into a chair. "That was fortunate. It could have been much worse, so I will say again how very sorry I am that I interfered with your friends and their spells." She held her breath.

Mara flapped a hand in her direction. "I really wish you hadn't, but what's done is done and you should know by now I don't hold grudges. In fact, *you* should know me well enough to trust me, but you didn't. That hurt, Brynn."

Brynn hung her head and picked at the donut half on her plate. "I was hurt also, when you were spending so much time with them and excluding me. We were the ones always together and then that stopped."

Brynn suddenly remembered Mara's accusation that Brynn had thought she needed rescuing because she was a human—was it true? Would Brynn have deferred to another Fae, instead of deciding she knew better and blundering in like a troll?

Mara put her hand on Brynn's, keeping her from spreading donut crumbs on the table. "It was only temporary, Brynn, and I'm sorry if I got caught up with my old friends. I wanted them to myself for a little while but I didn't know you cared that much."

Brynn thought of Avery's advice to make her feelings plain to Mara, to not allow any room for misinterpretation.

"But you would have known how much I cared by now, if I was not so wary of ruining our friendship. As I have not yet spoken outright of my feelings for you, let me do so now: Mara, I would like us to be more than friends. Lovers, if you are of like mind."

Mara gaped at her, struck speechless for the moment. As the silence grew, Brynn was tempted to take it all back, to say it was a joke. But humans did not live long so their time together would be limited—Brynn was feeling greedy and wanted all the time with Mara that she could have.

Mara's lips opened and closed a few times before she said, "Okay."

She said it so flatly that Brynn thought at first she was hearing a rejection. Then she realized the word had been "okay" and Mara was agreeing. But Brynn had laid her heart bare and surely she should get more than one word in return?

"So you care for me also?" Brynn prompted.

"Yes," Mara sighed, again sounding less enthusiastic than Brynn expected.

"Should I go buy a sympathy card for you then?" Brynn was getting the hang of dry humor.

"What?" Mara stopped looking inward at whatever conflict Brynn's words had created inside her, and finally paid attention to Brynn properly. Her eyes softened and Brynn began to believe Mara did feel the same about her. "I'm sorry, I'm not making this easy, am I? It's just that—I lost a lot during the Border's destruction and the Shifting afterwards.

My parents and my family didn't make it. Since then, if I start to get close to anyone my mind skips ahead to what it will be like to lose them.

"I dated Fae exclusively for a while, thinking at least they wouldn't die on me so easily. But it turns out when they voluntarily leave it hurts pretty bad, too. They didn't think about the relationship the same way—humans were not equals to them. Not like you seem to treat us. You came into my life after I'd decided it was better to keep everyone at arm's length so I never have to go through any of that again. Friends were okay, but nothing more serious."

"So you have a lot of friends but not many genuine relationships? What about Riley?" Brynn challenged.

"She burrowed her way into my heart like an annoying tick. I never meant to love her—or you."

"In summary, you love me and I am another annoying parasite? Beware, I shall swoon at such flattery."

Mara laughed, and Brynn could see tension leaving her body. She looked more like her merry self again, and less like a person dwelling in painful memories. Mara leaned over and kissed Brynn, communicating all the things she could not—or would not—say aloud.

Then Riley came running into the kitchen. "Did I miss the donuts? I had to go to the bafroom—"

She broke off her words as Brynn and Mara pulled apart.

Mara whispered, "To be continued," and Brynn nodded. All her panic about whether Mara would reject her had disappeared with that kiss, and she could wait for more. Not patiently, mind you, but she would wait.

Riley was still staring at them with narrowed eyes and Mara's smile faltered. *Oh no—if Brynn has to go against the child's wishes, then Mara's affections are not secured yet after all.*

"Who kissed who first?" Riley demanded.

Brynn and Mara exchanged glances and Mara said, "It's whom. I kissed her. Why do you need to know?"

"Whom got all talky first?" Riley asked, as if Mara had not answered her.

"I confessed my feelings first, if that is what you mean," Brynn replied.

They were not prepared when Riley let out a whoop and ran out to the garden. "Aurora! You win the first pool but I got the second! You all owe me a dozen cupcakes, and I know it didn't say on the sign up sheet but I meant a dozen cupcakes from each of you if I win."

"There was a sign up sheet for cupcakes?" Brynn asked. "Why was I not given the chance at free sweets?"

"No, they were betting on us," Mara explained. "On whether we'd hook up, and it sounds like Aurora and Riley guessed right. They won."

"Oh, I think it is us 'whom' have won—though the rewards will happen later. Speaking of which, would you like to come over to my apartment tonight?"

Mara laughed and her face went red, but her eyes kindled with anticipation. "Well, I mean I was going to anyway so I could talk to You-Know-Who about a plan for what we should do next. But I'll get the pooka to suggest a game night so Riley will stay home."

Brynn kissed Mara's palm and they went on to separate tasks to prepare for their date; Brynn wanted to stop by the marketplace and get some ingredients for a special dinner. She had recently been introduced to the joys of something called pesto and wanted to make a huge bowl of pasta to share with Mara. And Avery could have some by herself in the second bedroom.

Before she left, Brynn checked with Aurora to see if she had any peppertini plants growing since she had an inkling its leaves would add some spice to the pesto.

"I do," said Aurora, "but I don't think humans can eat it safely. I have some of the herbs humans like: basil, oregano, thyme, and cinnamon. Would those work?"

Brynn narrowed her eyes at Aurora. "You are not trying to sabotage me, are you? Even I know cinnamon does not belong in pesto."

"Of course I'm not sabotaging you and Mara, or I would have let you have the peppertini leaves. It's not poisonous to humans and would only give them an upset stomach. The cinnamon was a joke. I wouldn't have let you actually put it in the dinner—but would you like to try a little cardamom in place of black pepper?"

After tasting a few grains of cardamom, Brynn agreed to try it. She left with bundles of herbs and a mortar and pestle, gifts from Aurora to celebrate her winning one of the betting pools. That meant Brynn only had to buy some cheese, nuts, and pasta at the marketplace. It took her a while longer because she also decided to pick out a fine wine and some cut flowers. By the time she finished, the bags were a little unwieldly and she wished she still had use of the rickshaw.

She could have left some parcels and come back for them, but instead Brynn stubbornly carried all of them, though the handles of the bags were cutting off all feeling in her hands. She reached Mrs. Dibbs's building and sighed with relief as she dropped half her load in the foyer. It would be no concession to make two trips up the stairs.

The scent of the herbs was pungent in her nostrils as she braced the bag against the doorjamb and struggled to unlock the deadbolt on her apartment. She nearly fell inside as the door gave way but Brynn caught herself.

"It is only me," she called. "If you could come take these bags from me then I will go fetch the others."

Silence and an empty living room greeted her. Brynn frowned and went into the kitchen to set the bags down; abandoned on the counter was a half-made peanut butter and jelly sandwich. The jars were still cool so they had not been out of the refrigerator long.

"A—Cally?" Brynn called, belatedly remembering she should not use Avery's real name. She moved into the hallway and no sounds came from the bathroom or either bedroom. Closing her eyes, she tried to use her aural senses to see if anyone else was in the apartment but nothing disturbed the silence.

Avery was gone—after Mara had entrusted her to take care of her. And as much as it could impact their fragile new start, Brynn would have to tell Mara. She hurried over to the phone and paused as she saw the blinking light on her answering machine. She pressed the play button.

"You hold that button down—yes, the one that says Memo—and then talk. See the blinking light? That means it's recording." It was Avery's voice, but so flat and monotone that Brynn barely recognized it.

"It will repeat what I say later?" That voice made Brynn gasp over Avery's confirmation.

"Dear Sister," Brecon continued, "I arrived at your home determined to return you to Phoenix's care, even if I had to render you unconscious and drag you by your hair. Imagine my surprise when instead of my useless sister, I found a girl hiding in your bedroom. A girl who I recognized from her time at Court: one Avery Flynn. I can only think it was our mutual startlement which allowed me to bespell her before her wild magic could come to her defense.

"She is now under my control and is a greater prize than you could ever be. I will not need to bow my head to that brutish wyvern you were betrothed to any longer—or to anyone, with the ultimate weapon in my arsenal. I will contact you later, as I am curious as to how Avery Flynn came to be in your apartment. But first I shall hide her away somewhere secure, in case you or anyone else should be tempted to mount a rescue. And in case there is any doubt..."

Brynn held her breath as a silence followed, and then jumped when a scream sounded.

"I ordered her to cut herself and it is quite deep," Brecon said. "Know that she is under a geis to mortally wound herself if she sees you and I do not stop her with a countercommand. Keep that in mind, dear Sister."

The machine beeped to indicate that was the end of the recording. Brynn had to catch herself on the edge of the counter to keep from collapsing, and that was how she spotted the bloodied knife on the floor. This was real, and she knew from experience Brecon was an expert on compulsion spells. After all, he had practiced some of them on her and they were excruciating even in the small moment it took her to cancel his spell.

Avery had no magic at all and would be as helpless as any normal human. The gods help her if Brecon found out her wild magic was not at his disposal. As Brynn finally stood again on her shaky legs, a sound at the door made her stagger backwards.

"Hey, are these your bags?" Mara asked. "They were down in the foyer and I thought maybe they were part of our dinner."

The bags thumped to the carpet as Mara caught sight of Brynn and her expression. "What is it? What's wrong?"

Without a word, Brynn reached over and played the message again.

16 Avery

I woke up and found I couldn't move; my eyelids worked and that was about it. My eyes faced into a corner where the walls weeped moisture and slime. A stench of decay overwhelmed my sense of smell—and taste, yuck. Who knew how long it had been since I had anything to eat or drink, but this place was a pretty effective appetite suppressant.

And apparently my being unable to move didn't mean I was unable to feel. My hip and shoulder ached on the side I was lying on, and one hand fritzed between numbness and hot pins since it was trapped under my body. The other arm had a spot of throbbing heat, like a fresh cut. Yet, everything was also weirdly distant, like I could observe things but they had no real impact on my emotions. I knew they should, though.

Footsteps approached and I quickly closed my eyes.

"You may stand and face me," a voice said.

I couldn't help the little moans of pain as my stiff self lurched to my hands and knees, and then to my feet. I caught glimpses of a wrecked room as I turned: wet drywall slumped at the foot of a stone wall, strips of insulation drooping from the ceiling like overcooked lasagna noodles. Something which might have once been a sofa to my right? Like a basement gone to rot and ruin.

I came to a stop in front of my captor and recognized him from Court; I had been too busy succumbing to his spell to put it together until now. Brynn's brother was Lord Brecon, who was always on the edges of the queen's council, whispering manipulations and lies. One of the bad guys I'd kept my distance from—unless his spell ordered me to do otherwise, ugh.

Skipping any pleasantries, Brecon held up something and asked, "Do you know what this is?"

It was difficult to make out at first in the dim light, but then I recognized the shape of intertwined spikes. I stubbornly wanted to play dumb, but his magic made me answer robotically. "It's a crown of thorns. Queen Maeve was going to put one on Lonan to make sure I obeyed her."

He nodded. "I remembered, and that is where I got the idea. This one is to make sure Lonan does as I say also, but I have made a few modifications. Shall I show you?"

When I didn't answer, he pulled the puppet string of his spell and made me nod. He looked around and fished a filthy basketball out of the debris.

Brecon reached out with the crown of thorns and it expanded in his hands, looking less like a crown and more like a bizarre corset. It fitted itself around the middle of the basketball, sizing to hug it without piercing.

"Now on a person, this would be their neck instead. You see, do you not?"

At my nod, he commanded, "So, try to remove it."

My hands jumped to do his bidding, and as soon as they approached it the crown constricted. The basketball burst into rubbery chunks and the fetid air from inside it blew past my face. No blood obviously, but it was way too easy for my imagination to add that to the scenario. But again, the most that made me feel was, "Huh. So that happened."

Then it was just the crown of thorns lying there, and Brecon smiling smugly.

"I needed you to see for yourself, so you can make a convincing case of the consequences to Lonan." When I still didn't react, he frowned for a moment. "Ah, my apologies. You are under a quiescent spell so you were easier to handle, but it will keep your emotions walled off. Is that better?"

Whatever he did, it did *not* make it better. A flood of deferred emotions hit me faster than I could process: fear, worry for Lonan, hating that I was so vulnerable as a human, etc swept over me until I was caught up.

I begged, "You're going to put it on Lonan? Don't, please—"

"You misunderstand. You are going to put it on yourself."

I couldn't misunderstand that and my mind reeled in horror as I picked up the crown, seeing it expand as it passed over my head—in front of my eyes and barely scraping my nose—and it embraced my neck. My hands fluttered, unsure if they should drop it or keep touching it.

"Leave it. It will only react now if you try to touch it with intent—but it will react instantaneously. Especially if anyone else tries to interfere with it. Plus, it has something like a dead man's switch built in if anything happens to me. Do keep that in mind, won't you?"

When I nodded, I half-expected the thorny crown to take it as a threat and pop my head off like a kid with a dandelion: *Mama had a baby but the head popped off.* Fortunately, my involuntary shudder didn't trigger it either.

"Now, you will follow me," Brecon said, and I did, right up the rickety stairs into daylight.

Along with the return of my feelings, he'd let my inner snark loose again. *What a conversationalist this guy is. Why is everything he says an order or a complaint? That must get so boring.* But my self-preservation wasn't limited to mocking him secretly; it also wanted to find a way to escape Brecon and his control.

I looked back at where he had hidden me and saw we were in a ruined part of Crow's Rest. Probably one of the older houses, since it had had a basement and stone foundation. Maybe if I could figure out where we were, I could trick Brecon into falling into a pit or something?

Oh right, that dead man's switch thing was connected to the CoT. So maybe I won't try and mess him up after all.

It turned out we weren't going very far anyway. Some glowing lights marked a pocket of Faerie up ahead, and Brecon was making straight for it—which meant, so was I. We must still be within the boundaries of Spellmeet if this pocket was active; any other areas of Faerie which ended up outside Spellmeet in the Shifting were dead-magic spots. Not spots for necromancy, I mean, just that the magic died in them. Like that rainbow forest in Ohio which was perfectly normal by human standards, except for the vivid colors of the plants.

Our destination was an island of Fae magic with a meadow of flowers, lit with sprites and the glowing windows of gnomes' houses. An outpost, but still connected to Faerie so probably great for smuggling. But it wouldn't matter if we took some back door into Faerie: Nykur had told me some pretty serious spells were set up to let everyone know Avery Flynn was back.

Would any of them trigger the crown, though? And was that scenario still better than Brecon using me against Lonan? *Nah, I'd better make sure my captor knows about the spells.*

"You know I can't sneak into Faerie, right? A lot of Fae want to get their revenge on me—"

"I know about the alarms," he interrupted. "In fact, I'm counting on them."

He grabbed my arm and took me with him, over the boundary into Faerie.

Shrieking alarms, ringing bells, bursts of light—all for little ol' me. Thankfully, my neck decoration didn't react, but Brecon seemed to be waiting for something. Or someone, as he ignored the Fae who transported near us and brandished weapons. It wasn't until we were surrounded by armored warriors—the Host—that Brecon spoke.

"Avery Flynn is my prisoner of war and all the rules and conditions apply. None may take her from me but the ruler of Faerie."

Was that true? Because Lonan would totally take me from him. I smiled to myself, ignoring the angry cries of the other Fae.

Brecon leaned in and whispered, "Do not get your hopes up. Will he exercise his rights when he knows I can trigger the crown of thorns from afar? I think not."

I sighed; Lonan would definitely not take the risk. Maybe once we talked, he could find a way around this deadly choker. But if Brecon thought the Host were just going to obey his demands for an escort to Court, he was mistaken. The guy in charge seemed to think it would be better to kill me and bring my corpse to the king.

I even had the dark thought that maybe I should let them kill me, since being vulnerable to Fae magic at Court was not going to go well for me. Last time I was human and in the queen's hands—when I spent time in that dungeon I'd slipped up and mentioned to Brynn—I had nearly died. Burned up from the inside out from gorging on Fae, glamoured food which could never truly nourish me. I had only stopped worse things from happening because I had my wyvern-side to call on; without it and my wild magic, I was defenseless—and able to be used as a pawn, like Brecon had already clued into.

Before I could test whether I could run at a sword, Brecon turned on his charm (and turned up his glamour). "King Lonan would not be happy if you denied him a reunion. Be assured I have Avery Flynn completely under my control and she is not a danger. The king will want to see that for himself."

Brecon's claim on me as a prize of war must have specific conditions in Fae law, because he ultimately won the argument for keeping me alive. The Host transported us to a spot outside the physical area of the Court buildings, the closest anyone could magically travel without triggering defenses. We had to walk down a long pathway through the grounds, which looked very different from when I was here last.

Granted, I had been flying away from a huge magical fire I had set, but I didn't think that fire was responsible for the craters and scorch marks pocking the grassy areas. I didn't think it was damage from the Shifting, either. It looked more like there had been a battle among the topiary and knot gardens. Or maybe some dragons fought here?

Either way, it did not inspire confidence in the stability of the rulers in the palace. Was the turnover really as bad as Nykur had said, and Lonan was a big walking target now? And would allegedly having Avery Flynn's wild magic under control help or hinder his rule? *I guess we're about to find out.*

As we passed groups of Fae Courtiers, cries of anger and distress followed us—until there were so many that the sounds traveled ahead of us, echoing from all the marble surfaces. It reminded me of all the other times I'd been in this cold, vast mausoleum to ask Queen Maeve for help or to apologize for something I'd done wrong. *Way more often for the latter.*

But this time it was Lonan who waited for us, looking right at home on a throne with his black garb and a stern expression. In spite of his usual self-control when he was doing royal stuff, his hand reached towards me before he caught himself and dropped back into an indifferent slouch.

"Avery," he said coldly. "It's been a while."

Was that a hint he'd told everyone we'd gone our separate ways after the Shifting? Or that our few days apart had felt like a lifetime to him too? *I'd better play along and see where he leads me in the conversation.*

"Your majesty," I said with an awkward curtsy. "How're they hanging?"

Someone in the crowd giggled, in such a high pitch that it was barely audible to humans. The sound hit me like nails dragging up my spine and I shuddered.

"They are hanging well, thank you," Lonan answered with a straight face, before he turned to Brecon. "Thank you for delivering Avery to your king."

Brecon bowed. "Of course, Your Majesty. But if I may clarify, Avery Flynn is still under my control as my prize of war."

Lonan started to speak but Brecon held up his hand. That alone made a few Host draw their swords, but Lonan inclined his head so my captor could continue.

"Your Majesty, there is a discussion we need to have in private. Would you allow this?"

Instead of answering right away, Lonan's eyes flickered to me. I gave the barest nod and Lonan's face tightened. *Here's hoping he doesn't think this is some escape ploy by me and he slings a spell in my direction—or Brecon's.*

Lonan led us to a smaller chamber off to the side of the throne room, rather than trying to clear out the larger room. I had been in here once during Queen Maeve's reign and only small details—the breakable pieces—of the décor had changed through however many rulers.

King Lonan gestured to some comfy-looking chairs near a fire and all three of us sat.

Before Lonan could speak, Brecon asked, "Are you sure we are quite alone? I only ask since I myself was a—an informant for the queen and I remember several secret access points to this room. I give my word that I do not mean to harm you, and that you will not want our conversation overheard."

Lonan stared at him for a moment and waited for my small nod again; his regal hand gesture did not seem to be directed to anyone in particular, but one tapestry fluttered slightly as if a door had closed behind it.

"We are alone now," Lonan said. "Avery, what's going on? It's too dangerous for you here."

I tried to reply but my lips wouldn't obey me; all I could do was make muffled cries. Lonan started to stand, but Brecon's laugh stopped him.

"My mistake. I left my command in place to prevent her from speaking. Let me lift it and she can answer you."

I gasped as I was able to move my mouth again. "Okay, first thing you need to know is you can't try any magic against Brecon and his control without this thing on my neck popping me like a tick. Do you understand?"

When Lonan nodded, I caught him up with what had happened: Brynn stashing me in her apartment, Brecon coming to drag his sister back to a wedding with Phoenix but finding me instead, and Brecon realizing I had no defense against his spells. Him making me cut myself to prove I was under his power.

"And then everything went black for a while. I'm guessing that's when he refined his nefarious plans."

"If it's the throne you want, Brecon, it may not be as easy to take as you think," Lonan said. "Many powerful families are invested on keeping me in power to enforce alliances—"

"I am not so foolish as to want the throne—along with a target on my back," Brecon interrupted. "I know I am not the Sovereign, and it is obvious neither are you. I have come to believe the true power is behind the throne, and that is the role I covet for myself."

"What makes you think I will go along with this?" Lonan asked.

"Besides the threat to your lover? You forget I was watching from the shadows as you grew up under Queen Maeve's rule. She punished you several times for being so outspoken against her treatment of humans and of her own subjects. Your idealism is well known, and you now have the opportunity to bring your beliefs into practice, through Fae law and diplomatic policies."

Lonan scoffed. "And you are helping me with this because you share my beliefs? I do not remember you ever speaking out against Queen Maeve's cruel streak."

"I assure you, I have my own goals, including restoring wealth and power to my family. But if Faerie is also assured a long and peaceful reign under you, how can you say no?"

I answered, "Like this: no."

Lonan and Brecon ignored me, caught in a staring contest with each other.

Lonan stood and paced. "You expect me to believe you will let Avery go?"

"I'm afraid that is not part of the bargain. She needs to be here in Court, on display to prove I was able to overpower her and her wild magic. Acknowledging my feat makes your appointment of me as a trusted advisor that much more believable.

You would rather she is close to you, would you not, Your Majesty?"

"Close to you, you mean, so you can see the bloodbath if something goes wrong with my magical collar," I muttered.

Brecon showed his teeth in a grin. "As I said, it is possible for my goals and the king's to align."

Lonan sighed. "That's what you want? For me to be your puppet king, and to parade a tamed Avery Flynn at Court?"

There was that hideous smile on Brecon again. "Merely one more thing, but it will not be a hardship. You might wish to sit down for this, King Lonan."

17 Brynn

After Brecon's voice stopped and the answering machine reset to the beginning, Mara fumbled onto one of the barstools and asked, "So where would your brother take Avery?"

Brynn picked up the bags of groceries as she thought, before saying, "He would have a much harder time keeping her presence a secret in Faerie, so I do not think he would take her there until he had planned for every eventuality. If he is hiding—and holding—her with magic, he would need to be in an actively magical region of Spellmeet for his spells to work. Do you have any way to find Avery or contact her?"

"We were very careful to contact each other through intermediaries. Nykur might be able to find her but I don't have a way to contact him directly either. Unless...maybe the Wild Hunt would help? I have an in with them."

Brynn stopped stowing groceries long enough to stare at Mara. How did a human have a way to connect with the Wild Hunt? "What do you mean? Do they owe her a favor? If not, the Wild Hunt would be more likely to call down justice on Avery than do your bidding. They might listen to Lonan if he has assumed the throne by now, however."

"Trying to get Lonan's okay might attract too much attention, anyway. It's not really the Huntsmen I know, but it's easier to show you. I hope you're up for spending our date night in a cemetery?"

Brynn started to argue on whether it was wise to have anything to do with the Wild Hunt—after all, they were so ancient and unknowable that only the Sovereign dared deal with them—but then she wondered if this was a situation where questioning her human lover might cause more friction between them. Better to give the benefit of the doubt and see how this played out.

They packed a quick to-go meal into one of the milk crates Mara kept in her rickshaw and climbed aboard it. The trip was not long but the late hour meant the roads were emptier than usual. The cemetery backed up to some woods and whispering trees loomed over the headstones.

It might have been unnerving, but their pool of lantern light was cozy with a blanket spread out. Cozy enough that Mara folded her jacket beneath her head and laid back.

"We have a few hours until midnight so we don't have to hurry to eat," Mara said. "We may as well find something else to do, or I'll worry the whole time."

"I can think of something," Brynn replied, and pounced on Mara (just as she had intended). Mara giggled into her neck as they rolled and tried not to squish the baguette.

They lost such track of time that the pounding of distant hooves like a bass drum shocked them from their tangle of limbs.

"Is that the Wild Hunt?" Brynn asked breathlessly.

"Yes!" Mara scrambled to her feet, fixing her clothing. "You won't want to miss this."

She pulled Brynn to the well-worn road leading from the woods and along the boundary of the cemetery. They perched on a stone wall under streetlights, waiting as the hooves grew louder.

Now the Hounds started baying too, making the hairs rise on the back of Brynn's and Mara's necks.

Fae and humans had both been hunted by this otherworldly pack for eons, and their skins and bones remembered.

The mass of huge dogs, roiling with so many legs and gaping jaws you could not pick out a single Hound, got closer. Brynn and Mara had to fight every instinct to stay in place, but before they knew it the Hounds had rushed past. Freshly churned mud marked their passage, some of which had splattered onto Brynn and Mara.

Next was the line of Huntsmen, variations on a theme of ancient, horned skulls and tousled fur. Their horses laid back long ears and slowed, until droplets of their sweat spattered the mud. Each Huntsman turned a fiery eye towards where Brynn and Mara clasped each other in terror, but then continued on his way. The light from the street lamps was empty again.

"They did not stop," Brynn cried, her voice too loud as the hooves still rang in her ears.

"Wait for it..." Mara replied.

A moment later, excited barks echoed in the woods. Like a siren, it sounded higher in pitch as it grew closer—and the dark, round body of a knee-high dog exploded onto the road. His smaller paws ate up the gravel and he would have continued on the trail of his packmates, but his nose came up and he skidded to a stop.

Mara stepped over to pet him but before she could touch his panting form, the dog dodged her and ran to their forgotten dinner. The sound of tearing aluminum foil was covered by trotting hoofbeats, and Mara and Brynn turned back to the woods.

A cloaked figure bounced on the back of a seal-colored pony, whose trot looked neither speedy nor comfortable for the rider. The pony was so out of place there was no possibility it could be part of the Wild Hunt—but for the curving hunting horn hung from the saddle.

The pony slowed as it came upon the churned mud and the rider called, "Bobbin? Where did you get to?"

"He's probably snout-deep in our dinner," Mara called.

The rider squinted against the brightness of the streetlights. "Missa! I mean, Mara, oops."

"Mara is good. Hi, Daniel."

Brynn knew she had heard that name in connection to Avery Flynn before—but not with blame attached to the name, as in Lonan's case. Had Daniel always been a Huntsman though? He dressed like the young humans who came into Spellmeet and treated magic like one of the elaborate games they played. They usually learned quickly that lives or injuries did not regenerate in Spellmeet.

Daniel dismounted and gave Mara a hug while the pony waded into the roadside weeds, already chewing.

"Are you hungry for human food?" Mara asked, leading Daniel to their picnic.

But when they found Bobbin, bits of foil were the only evidence of the bread, cheese, and salami. Their cries of dismay only made him eat faster, in case they were going to take it away. Thankfully Bobbin could not work the zipper on the small cooler.

"Doesn't that dog ever get full?" Mara asked with a sigh. "The only thing left is wine and figs, I guess."

Daniel was happy to join them and once they each finished their handful of fruit, Mara asked, "How are your parents, Daniel? Are they still okay?"

"As long as they stay in Faerie, the magic countering the botulism keeps them alive. My dad wanted to risk going to the funeral of a friend but Mom talked him out of it; she didn't want to have a funeral for him too. They seem happy enough otherwise, and have made a few friends with other expats in Faerie."

Daniel and Mara continued chatting, and Brynn rubbed the very full belly of Daniel's dog, until Mara asked him, "Have you heard anything from our friend lately?"

"Not lately," Daniel said. "I've been pretty busy with the Hunt."

Bobbin groaned in disappointment as Brynn's attention turned back to the humans.

"How did you become involved with the Hunt?" she asked.

"It was Bobbin: he chased after the Hunt one night, and I went after him on Otter. Otter was a pasture pony but it turned out he was up for an adventure too. We finally caught up to the Hunt a few nights later and they let us join them.

"The Huntsman don't talk to us much but we're...comrades, I guess. Packmates or herdmates or something."

Mara laughed. "Like mascots?"

Daniel turned red and laughed. "Maybe at first, but I have an actual role now. You know how the legends about the Wild Hunt say they hunt souls?

He waited until Brynn and Mara nodded before he continued, "The souls are lost in the twilit in-between, and may not even know they've died. We do hunt them, but what we do with them once they are cornered depends on how they lived their lives.

"Most of them are herded right into the afterlife, like sheep passing through a gate and into a fresh, green pasture. And some are run down, literally *hounded* until they have paid a price for their misdeeds before they move on.

"Then there are the children. Not surprisingly, a lot of the kids aren't okay with creepy deer skulls looming at them. And as much as I love dogs, those Hounds can be scary as—well, they can be terrifying.

"I convinced the Hunt of the advantages of having someone more approachable handle the kids who need help moving on. That if they're not scared out of their wits, they can better face the next stage of their journeys. I was good with the terminal kids when I volunteered at the hospital, so this was like a natural extension of that."

"Plus, you basically look like Tom Bombadil in that getup, with your fuzzy pony and dizzy little dog," said Mara. "Less beard, though."

Daniel laughed. "Yeah, there is that."

But as their laughter faded, Mara and Brynn exchanged a glance.

"You weren't overcome with nostalgia and needed to see me, were you?" Daniel asked.

Mara shook her head. "It's—our mutual friend is in trouble. She's missing."

Daniel sighed. "You think she's in trouble with the Hunt?"

"Not exactly. We need help finding her and I thought the Hunt could be just the ticket."

"Believe me, you don't want their attention. They noticed you when they passed by, and even that was unusual. Unless it's someone they are hunting, ordinary people may as well be trees to them. If they interact with someone—single them out—it doesn't end well for the human."

"Perhaps they were looking at me?" Brynn mused. "Carregs are rare and it is possible the Wild Hunt are no more fond of one than my own people are."

A horn sounded in the distance and Daniel muttered, "Oh, shit. I think you're about to find out why the Huntsmen were looking at you. They're circling back."

The hounds were on them first, ringing Brynn and Mara with their frenetic motion. Heated dog breath enveloped them and Mara clutched tighter to Brynn.

A smaller female hound, with her beard and face white where the others' were foxy-red, came to sit in front of them expectantly. Smaller was a relative term as her head came to their waists instead of their shoulders. Her soulful eyes stared up at

Brynn—was she waiting for a pat on the head? Or waiting for one of them to reach out a hand so she could bite it off and add it to her collection?

Daniel said, "She likes to have her ears rubbed."

Mara and Brynn each picked an ear to rub and the hound went boneless, letting out a groan like an old man reaching for a penny on the sidewalk.

"Is that a happy sound?" Mara asked doubtfully.

"Yeah, it is," Daniel answered. "She's just old—maybe the oldest of the ancient hounds—and she makes noises like a creaky door. But she's the one who calls the pack to the Hunt every night and you can see it then—she must have been magnificent when she was younger."

Brynn looked into the aged hound's eyes and they were not merely soulful—entire galaxies bloomed and faded in their depths. "She still is magnificent."

Brynn felt the tiniest touch of a tongue on her hand before the old girl rejoined the pack and made room for the arriving Wild Huntsmen.

Mud sprayed from beneath the horse's hooves, with the spatter hitting Brynn and Mara's clothes. It was not the time to protest, however, so they did their best to surreptitiously wipe off the stains.

Brynn looked up to see that one of the Huntsmen was pointing a bony finger directly at her. It spoke to her in the language of the Fae, but with some indiscernible accent. Or perhaps it was a primitive form of the tongue?

Mara did not seem to understand, but Daniel's expression made Brynn think he had caught the meaning.

"I am summoned to Court," Brynn said for Mara's benefit. "The king himself has ordered it."

"Oh!" Mara said. "Do you think Lonan—His Majesty—knows where our friend is?"

Brynn tried to ask what the summons was about, but the Huntsman only stared at her with his ember-bright eyes smoldering in their sockets of bone.

"They're not big on explanations," Daniel explained. "They give instructions once and you'd better be paying attention."

"Maybe we can send a note first," Mara said. "I don't like the idea of going into Court with no idea what we are walking into."

"I have no choice but to appear. I cannot ignore my king."

Mara snorted. "He's not my king. I've ignored him on several occasions, so I can teach you."

Brynn smiled but shook her head. "I must go. Even now I feel the pull of it."

"Okay, but let's stop by my house first so I can get some things. And I need to make sure someone keeps an eye on Riley—"

"No need," Brynn interrupted. "You are not included in the summons."

Mara stared hard at her before saying, "Well, put me down as your plus one because I'm going with you. I'm not helpless."

Brynn pulled Mara further away so she could whisper, "I know you are not helpless, and that is why I do not want you to come with me. As you say, we do not know what I am walking into."

"Exactly—" Brynn cut off her words with a kiss. Instead of making Mara soften as she thought it would, it made her look more stubborn.

Brynn squeezed her hand. "I am sorry to cut off your argument with a kiss, but please know that the Huntsmen can whisk me away at any moment. It is important I say some things, including that if you genuinely want to help, you are better placed outside the Court. If this is a trap as we both fear, am I correct that you could call in some favors on my behalf? Not enough to get me released perhaps, but enough to cause trouble for the king?"

When Mara just stood there frowning, Brynn put some space between them. "I understand if you do not want to risk yourself or your friends and family."

Mara grabbed Brynn and kissed her fiercely before whispering, "You are family. You are not getting rid of me that easily."

Brynn pressed a kiss on the corner of Mara's lips. "I am counting on it."

And before either of them could say anything else, Brynn was swept up in a flurry of horse's hooves and springing hounds as they carried her off to Court. Mara and Daniel exchanged a very human, dread-filled glance before going their separate ways into the night.

18 Brynn

It was difficult for Brynn to judge how long it might take them to get to Court since the surroundings were a featureless blur from the rush of the horse's jarring strides. Did these mounts have any other speeds besides full gallop and standstill? Or was the pace a reflection of the urgency of her summons?

The Huntsman who had pulled Brynn up behind him seemed to be ignoring her and she was grateful for the time to think. She hoped Mara would not put herself in danger on her behalf, but her declaration that Brynn was family had sounded unshakable. Brynn allowed herself a moment to revel in the warm feeling that gave her before she turned her mind to more serious matters.

What could King Lonan want with her? Was it anything to do with Avery's disappearance? If the king had good news on that front he could have sent a message far more easily than organizing the Wild Hunt to collect her.

Perhaps he needed her carreg powers for a Courtly task? But again, "Starling" had seemed more the type to ask for her help than to demand it. Brynn could not quite shake the prickly, worrisome feeling there was something more sinister behind this summons.

The horse seemed to be slowing beneath her so it should not be long before she found out. The passing blur resolved into distinct trees and the remains of Queen Maeve's torturous rose hedge. The Huntsman lifted her down, bracing her until she found her feet. Then he stared at her meaningfully.

"Thank you?" Brynn tried.

But he continued to gaze at her and Brynn remembered a phrase she had heard Mara say to an overexcited Riley.

"Use your words like a sensible person," she said to the Huntsman.

He scoffed before wheeling his horse and galloping away. Not very helpful, but Brynn had more weighty things to ponder than what he had been trying to communicate.

As she started up the path, a handful of the Host came out to meet her. She returned their bows with a curtsy and they continued as a group. Were they surrounding her to keep her from fleeing, or as some sort of honor guard? It was all very peculiar.

It became even more peculiar as the large doors opened before her and the crowd inside stopped their chattering to bow or curtsy before her. Not ever having been to Court before, Brynn had no idea if this was the usual greeting, or whether she was expected to return each courtesy. A nod seemed to be sufficient, although whispers spread in her wake.

Under other circumstances, the sounds of so many spells would have overwhelmed her, but she was too focused on walking up the long, flowered carpet without tripping. As she approached the dais, the king himself stood and descended the stairs. This time she knew a curtsy was the right greeting.

"Welcome, Lady Brynn. Thank you for answering my call."

Through her lowered eyelashes, Brynn searched Lonan's face for any clues to what was expected of her but his expression remained politely blank. Best to cooperate until they had a chance to speak privately.

But when he started to lead her up the stairs, she balked. There was no good reason for her to be that close to the thrones—and why were there two thrones? If Avery was at Court, should she not be beside the king?

It was not until Brecon stepped from the shadows, gesturing grandly for her to take her place in the smaller throne, that she felt her stomach drop. From the triumph hiding beneath his smile, he seemed to be the real person behind her summons. Her own smile felt applied with a heavy hand and she knew Avery—and most women—would recognize it as a protective shield.

Lonan helped her sit before taking his own place, and Brynn shifted subtly on the plush seat. It was not the red velvet cushion which was so uncomfortable—that honor belonged to all the sharp pieces of bone making up the arms and frame for the seatback. The bones were arranged to resemble stag horns, but the variety of sizes and shapes reminded the Court of the myriad of creatures who had died to make it.

If that was not concerning enough, an insect flew at her and droned next to her ear. Even as the Courtly chorus launched into an exultant song, she could hear the buzz.

She broke her semblance of calm to grab for the flying pest and as her hand got closer, she felt the aura of magic around it. *Was this a spy? Or an assassin?* She quickly used her magic to cancel the spell and something dropped into her lap.

Gingerly, she poked it with a fingertip and saw it was a small scroll of tightly wound paper. She looked around, but both Lonan and Brecon seemed to be paying rapt attention to the music. So she pretended she was doing the same, while her fingernails felt for an edge to unroll the missive.

In tiny, spidery script it read: *"Please go along with all this until we can speak privately and come up with another plan. Avery's life depends upon it."* The signature was a blackbird.

As she had no plan herself, nor any idea what was really going on, what choice did Brynn have but to follow the king's lead? She suppressed a sigh and slid the paper into her sleeve; she would dispose of it when she got the chance.

The music stopped and Brynn sat up straighter, feeling the attention of the Courtiers on her once again. She darted a glance at Lonan; anyone further away would only have seen his bored, distant facial expression, but she could see a question burning in his gaze. She gave him the slightest nod and he relaxed into a slouch.

Brecon knelt before King Lonan, asking, "May I be the one to deliver the happy news to your Court, Your Majesty?"

Lonan waved a hand imperiously in permission—and then placed his hand over Brynn's in a tender way. Brynn only just stopped herself from recoiling from his touch, reminding herself that he had asked her to "go along" with this spectacle.

Brecon gave a florid speech about how grateful he was to have the king's trust and a new position as his adviser. Since she had heard her brother glorify himself on many occasions, Brynn tuned him out and watched the Courtiers instead.

Most seemed to be making an effort to at least look like they were listening politely. But scattered throughout the crowd were a few skeptical expressions, or dismissive, or outright hostile ones. It appeared Brecon had yet to cement his place at Court, even if he was holding a threat over the king via Avery.

His seemingly casual mention that Brynn would be putting her carreg powers to work on behalf of her king was received with quickly stifled gasps. Raised fans could not entirely hide the consternation this announcement caused. Brecon's speech was building to a crescendo, leading Brynn to think her brother had a plan beyond becoming an advisor to the king—especially when she knew the royals who followed Queen Maeve had not held the throne long enough to suit Brecon's long-term ambitions.

She forced herself to smile and nod as Brecon's pacing brought him to her side, and his hand fell to her shoulder. It may have looked like an affectionate gesture, but his fingers dug painfully into her flesh. When he announced that his beloved sister would be marrying none other than Lonan, the King of Faerie, Brecon's hand was the only thing keeping her from leaping from her seat and fleeing the Court.

The cries of celebration sounded like ominous chords to her ears, but they did not keep her from hearing Lonan's low whisper as he leaned towards her. "Thank you for not denying me, Brynn. I will make sure we have a chance to speak soon."

An eternity passed while important Fae families minced past the dais to deliver their congratulations. Finally, Lonan stood and took her by the hand. He pointed a smoldering leer at her and she stopped a guffaw before it left her lips.

Lonan announced, "You will all understand I am eager to taste the charms of my beloved, so we will see you again anon."

The chorus launched into the opening chords of a popular love song: "If all the rivers turned to ice..."

Their voices faded as Lonan led her into a chamber off the throne room and shut the heavy wooden doors.

"What is happening—" Brynn started to ask, but Lonan cut her off.

"We only have a moment before Brecon and Avery join us, so please know I am not a willing participant myself. Your brother has a Crown of Thorns rigged to kill Avery if anyone tries to remove it or to harm him. Even reaching out with your carreg powers might be enough, so be cautious."

It was fortunate that Lonan had warned Brynn, because she would have instinctually reached out to see what power Brecon had over Avery when they joined them in the snug antechamber. As it was, magic swirled around Avery (including a spell which was obviously keeping her from speaking her mind) like a swarm of gnats and stoked her curiosity. Brynn nodded politely to Avery and they all took a seat.

Brecon launched into a summary of the wedding contract, which he had obviously already worked out to the smallest detail. Brynn sat in misery as his words washed over her.

He finished by saying, "Do not worry, you both will have time to get used to the idea since the ceremony is a few months away. That will also give the Court a chance to come up with appropriate gifts, and the pageantry might distract the uneasy elements from looking for the next in line for the throne."

He looked at his sister for any argument, expecting the contrariness she had shown at his last visit to her home. But she smiled sweetly and did not give him the satisfaction.

"It sounds delightful, Brother. May I have a moment alone with my betrothed? Or perhaps we should retire now, as my king hinted that there is no reason to delay our bedsport."

Brecon shook his head in disappointment. "Ah, Sister, do you really want to set the tone for our happy reunion by lying to me?"

"There is a difference between lying and mockery, Brother." Brynn sighed and continued, "If you and Lonan have some sort of agreement, do not count on me being a part of it."

Raising an eyebrow, Brecon asked, "And what of the danger to Avery Flynn? You used to be so softhearted when it came to humans."

Brynn sent an apologetic smile to both Avery and Lonan. "I have much empathy for Lonan and Avery getting caught in your plans, since I have been in the same spot before. I will help as much as I am able. But I have a life now, I have someone...I have plans of my own. You know what my life was like with our parents, Brecon—surely you can understand I want to make my own decisions now. I want to experience new things, not to be stuck at Court performing tricks."

Brecon's voice was soft when he answered, but Brynn knew that only masked his rage. "And what of the sacrifices the rest of our family has made? Do you know Father has retreated to his mountain and even now is ossifying? Mother is so shamed that she rarely leaves our home. Fae families far beneath us laugh at her, that her defective daughter would break a marriage contract. But announcing you and the king were secretly engaged will allow all of us to regain our rightful position and deference."

Brynn bit her lip; she knew she owed nothing to her awful family, but she would not leave Avery and Lonan to her brother's plans without making one more try.

"What if we compromised?" she asked after a moment to think. "I will play the part of dutiful fiancée for an agreed length of time. Then Lonan can find some reason to break it off, banishing me from Court or an equally drastic punishment—as long as it frees me from this marriage."

Lonan grasped at this plan like it was a lifeline. "That sounds reasonable to me. The Court will enjoy the drama of a breakup even more than the pageantry of a wedding."

Brecon shook his head. "For you to keep your throne, my king, you must have something on your side other than Avery Flynn's capture. Carreg magic—and with it, the ability to thwart even the most powerful spells—is the key to your reign being a long and peaceful one. I leave it to you both to decide if this will be a marriage in name only, but in public you must present a united front. Or I am afraid any agreement I have made with Lonan is null and void."

Before Brynn could reply, Lonan spoke. "We will not solve this tonight. Brecon, if Brynn and I can come up with another plan which does not involve marriage and her being shackled to Court, are you open to listening?"

Brecon's eyes flashed with triumph. "Of course— I am nothing if not reasonable. But in the meantime, I must insist you go through with our immediate plans. There is a ball tomorrow night and you both should be well-rested, and practiced at lingering looks, by then. And Sister, you will need a dress fitting since we cannot glamour an outfit for you."

Brynn considered—she could commit to a dress fitting and a ball, for now. Putting on a public face would only gain her more time to subvert Brecon's plans in private.

She nodded and said, "I do believe rest is a good next step. Where is my room, please?"

"You will share the king's rooms, of course, since it is expected." Brecon held up a hand before she could protest. "Do what you want behind closed doors, but I will not budge on this."

He started to walk away without waiting for an answer, but then turned back with a wicked smile. "Avery should join you, also. What better way to prove to all of you that even Brynn cannot save her from the Crown of Thorns? But do not test the spell too closely, or you will be caught in the blast as it explodes. I added another layer which will take out anyone within twenty feet—after it has dispatched Avery, of course."

At their unhappy expressions, Brecon laughed. "Do not worry, I just removed her silencing spell. Consider this a wedding gift, my king. What could be better than more time with your lover and your betrothed?"

"How about removing this collar altogether?" Avery muttered. "That would be something to celebrate."

"So droll. I will see all of you tomorrow." Brecon offered a cheery wave as he left. "And Sister, you may expect your wedding gift from me at the ball."

Why did that sound like a threat to Brynn?

19 Avery

"Does anyone else feel like they're not up to facing the crowds yet?" Lonan asked.

My hand shot up in the air and Brynn smiled hesitantly. *Hmm, I'll have to put in the effort to bring the princess over to the Dork Side.* Mara will thank me for it later.

Lonan beckoned us to follow as he opened a secret panel in the wall, leading to a stone passage that took us down steps, and past a few other doors, before climbing again and spitting us out through a hidden door in the king's rooms.

"Growing up in the palace as the queen's favorite nephew has its advantages," Lonan said as he sealed the edges of the door into invisibility again. "Not only do I know how to get around undetected, I know most of the places others can spy from."

"So we're not being watched in here?" I asked.

"No, the palace itself has safeguards in the royal apartment against that."

I screamed out loud and then called Brecon every bad word and name I could think of, until I started making things up. "And he's a radish-lover, as in he's sexually attracted to radishes—but it would traumatize you both too much to hear all the details."

Brynn and Lonan had laughed at my tirade, but as I was winding down Lonan asked, "Are you finished? What was that all about?"

"Without the silencing spell, it feels good to be able to talk again and say all the things I was thinking."

"Indeed?" Brynn looked interested. "Does that mean you can tell us about his secret plans?"

I shook my head. "The only ones he's bothered to share when I was around were the wedding plans, which I'm sure we will all be so sick of before the day even arrives."

Talking about the wedding made me sad—*and a little possessive, if I'm being honest*—so I went to hug Lonan. He held his arms at his side awkwardly, until I drew back to look at his face.

"I don't know what I can and can't do with that thing on your neck," he explained. "What if I go to touch your face or something and find myself touching a bloody neck stump instead?”

I shuddered. “Thank you for that romantic scenario. Brecon said the spell could sense intention, and only an attempt to affect the COT would trigger it.”

“Forgive me if I don’t trust the kidnapper,” Lonan said with a snort. “It’s not exactly something we can experiment with to find the boundaries, Avery.”

Brynn had collapsed on a chaise, so I went to sit by her and asked, “What about it, Brynn? Is your brother being truthful or tricksy about the spells he put on me?”

“Base your answer on what you know about him, please,” Lonan put in nervously, “not on checking the spell.”

Brynn yawned, but sat up to think before answering, “He is not above lying or tricking anyone, but I think in this case Avery is too valuable as leverage for him to leave her safety in doubt. However, once we are safely married and he feels more secure in the king’s loyalty, I suspect that will change.”

“So this thing on me isn’t just a bomb, it’s a ticking time bomb.” I mused. “Well then, as the wedding comes closer, I vote we start to experiment. What will I have to lose at that point?"

Lonan sighed at my offhand tone, probably because he knew me well enough to recognize that when I was at my most glib, I was also at my most worried. But Brynn didn't know that, so it was sweet when she reached over to squeeze my hand.

"We will try to avoid that," she said. "In the meantime, would you like to know more about the magic around you?"

I said, "Yes!" the same time as Lonan cried, "No!" and Brynn smiled before she continued.

"I promise this has nothing to do with the Crown of Thorns and my brother's spells. It is more of a continuation of our conversation about wild magic, Avery."

I hadn't had a chance to speak privately with Lonan since I'd come to Court, so Brynn and I caught him up on what she'd told me before about the two wild magics.

"After Avery's encounter with the wings, I put some thought into other odd occurrences at Taylor's shop," Brynn said. "I believe many of those instances could have been wild magic trying to get my attention. The interruptions happened most often when I was concentrating very hard on repairing a piece of technology. I would be so deeply involved in what I was doing that I would let my carreg powers relax, since I did not need to pay attention to magic when working with a machine. Then, it would be like a toddler blowing a kazoo next to my ear and my attention would snap back to my surroundings and my magic."

"My wild magic is the kazoo in your story?" I asked. "And wait, you can set your powers aside and pick them up whenever you want?"

"Not exactly, no. I would say it was more like flexing and relaxing a muscle, or perhaps how we breathe automatically but can also choose to take control of our breaths."

Mindful magic. I chuckled at the thought, but Lonan spoke up.

"The way you are describing wild magic, it's like it has a mind of its own. I've only ever heard the royal magic described like it is a separate entity, but joined with its host."

Brynn and Lonan looked at me, and I guess I was the best person to answer that question, since I'd experienced both of them. I relished my time in the spotlight and dramatically paced across the elaborate throw rug before answering.

"That's mostly accurate, but it wasn't words so much as feelings or images shared between me and the royal magic. Like the magic and I felt things simultaneously. With my wild magic, it was more like another voice in my head, but only when I was connected to it—hosting it, I guess. Now, I don't think I'd have a clue if one of those magics was doing jumping jacks while reciting terrible poetry right in front of me."

Brynn started and said, "As soon as you mentioned that, the wild magic sounded like a marching band bouncing around the room. It can obviously hear and understand you, even if the reverse is not true."

I looked around, but I genuinely couldn't hear or feel anything. I called, "Hello? I've missed you. I didn't mean to let Merlin use you like that. Do you forgive me?"

We all waited for some response, but again Brynn was the only one who could detect anything.

"It sounded like someone blowing a raspberry."

That startled a laugh out of me and then I asked, "Does it sound like it's coming from a specific part of the room?"

Before Brynn could answer, Lonan nodded. "That's a good thought."

Brynn asked, "Why does that matter?"

"Because we could come up with a simple binary—aka yes or no—system to ask it questions," Lonan answered. "That's what you were thinking, right, Avery?"

"Nerd," I scoffed. "I was actually thinking we could set up a Ouija board wherever the wild magic is, or maybe we could borrow an EVP recorder from the ghost-hunting team who used to set up at Warren Castle. Then create an elaborate language of sounds over the next few months, assuming we could hold its attention that long, and have real conversations with it. But sure, your simplified plan might work in the short term."

Lonan grinned back. "Why don't we try my stupid idea first and if it doesn't work, then we can look into getting your occult devices?"

"Deal. Brynn, do you think you'd be better able to tell the difference from two sounds or the same sound coming from different places?"

"Two sounds, definitely. But how will I know which meaning is intended?"

Lonan said, "We'll have to let it decide."

"O ye wilde magick, what sound doth signify 'no'?" I asked solemnly.

Brynn chuckled. "The raspberry sound again."

I shook my head. "I walked right into that one. Okay, what means 'yes'?"

"It sounds like a ringing bell."

Now that it was time to think of a question, my mind went totally blank. I opened and closed my mouth a few times and then shot Lonan a pleading look.

His wicked grin slipped out. "I guess we'll have to ask some test questions first, to establish how reliable this method is. Like a lie detector test. Wild Magic, does Avery sing bad pop music in her sleep?"

"Hey!" I cried. "That's not a real test question, bad music is subjective—"

But Brynn was laughing. "An emphatic yes."

I huffed at both of them. "Wild Magic, is Lonan likely to be in bed with me any time soon to confirm that?"

Brynn shook her head no, trying to suppress a smile.

"Oh, so now it can predict the future?" Lonan asked tartly.

Ignoring him, I said, "Okay, time to get serious. Wild Magic, were you attached to Merlin or me?"

Our interpreter frowned. "That was not a yes or no question."

"Okay. Were you Merlin's magic?"

Brynn shook her head. "Then it must be yours."

Lonan held up a finger. "Not necessarily. The confusion about Merlin's deeds and Avery's was all about everyone thinking only her wild magic was in play. We shouldn't assume that."

"True," I said with a sigh. "Wild Magic, were you my partner in crime?"

"I think it liked that description because lots of bells rang," Brynn replied.

"Speaking of descriptions, it feels stupid to keep calling it 'Wild Magic.' Maybe a name would be better? Too bad it can't tell us a name—that's where a Ouija board would come in handy."

Instead, Lonan and I took turns suggesting ridiculous names. Lonan's sounded like they were straight out of the dirty parts of the Urban Dictionary, while I threw out random words and sounds. Then Lonan really showed his bias and started listing birds—the magic settled on Magpie.

"Really?" I said. "Isn't that just another type of blackbird? I'll be outnumbered with Lonan and his family and now Magpie."

"Nope, magpies are black-and-white birds," Lonan blew a raspberry at me.

"Lonan and Magpie do speak the same language," Brynn said with a smile.

"Okay, Magpie it is," I said in surrender. "So Magpie, are you all caught up on what's happened so far?"

At Brynn's nod, I added, "I know it's a long shot, but do you have a plan to fix things since you're so clever?" *A little flattery couldn't hurt.*

Brynn shook her head, though, and she didn't offer up her own plan.

Lonan sighed and rubbed his feathery mane. "No worries, we have time to figure something out. For now, let's take advantage of a chance to eat well and sleep even better."

He knew to mention food first, even though I was a fan of sleeping too. Lonan had already sent for some human food for me, since we knew from experience that Fae food does a number on me when I'm fully human. A feast of all my favorite things was just what I needed.

Brynn waited until we all had eaten our fill before asking, "What are our sleeping arrangements? I do not have any reservations about sharing a bed with you two, but I am thinking of Mara. Would she be upset if she learned of it, Avery?"

"If you two haven't worked out the rules ahead of time, she might be, yeah. She's had more than one partner at a time but everyone knew and was okay with it. But you know you can sleep with us and not *sleep* with us, right?"

"Where is the sport in that?" Lonan and Brynn said at the same time, then laughed like it was an inside joke among the Fae. *Great, now they were bonding and I would be outnumbered again.*

I looked around Lonan's—the king's—chambers, never having been here when it was Queen Maeve's. The bed was plenty big enough for an orgy, but we'd already ruled it out. The chaise was the only other piece of furniture which looked comfortable enough to sleep on, since the interior designer must have loved Nordic interiors. The plush bed, velvet chaise, thick carpets, and painted cabinets were a huge difference from the rest of the palace.

We dragged the chaise into Lonan's vast walk-in closet for Brynn, and she closed the door with a grateful wave (despite her teasing me earlier). When Lonan and I climbed into bed, he seemed to still be giving me my space—or giving the COT its space, I guess.

He fell asleep right away but I laid awake for a while, thinking of Magpie and if we'd ever be reunited. That made me feel even lonelier and I scooted over to Lonan; he put an arm around me in his sleep and I didn't blow up, so that was a win.

I expected we would pick up with Magpie again the next morning, but apparently the wild magic was AWOL. Instead, the entire day was a whirlwind of dress fittings and preparations for the evening ball, since Brynn and I both needed real clothing.

Fortunately, Lonan had insisted my captor honored a few conditions of my presence at Court, like Brecon setting up a perimeter spell around me where I could not be glamoured. Even though no one realized I was without magic (hopefully), it wouldn't be out of character for a bored Fae to try to trick me into triggering the Crown of Thorns just for fun. Brecon was happy to fulfill Lonan's request because he also did not want his leverage to disappear without his say-so.

But the no-glamour zone meant I couldn't wear the latest magical fashions. A glamour would not hold on a carreg either, so Brynn was also getting a handmade garment. The human seamstresses relished the challenge of making a suitable gown for Brynn, whom everyone treated as if she was already the queen.

Spending the afternoon with the fiancée of my lover could have been awkward but it ended up being fun. I had liked Brynn already but it was obvious she hadn't trusted me when I first showed up in Spellmeet and was jealous of the time Mara spent with us. Now that we were more firmly on the same side, we discovered we could be friends. In fact, if not for the reminder of instantaneous death I wore around my neck, the time spent with Brynn and my girly side and elegant dresses would have been a perfect day.

My ballgown was wine-colored, with embroidered roses in the same colors so the pattern was subtle in most light. The bodice was actually a double-breasted jacket, almost military in its severe styling. The seamstress wanted to add gold epaulets and other ornamentation but I told her I wasn't going to the ball dressed as Sergeant Pepper.

To coordinate with Brynn's purple ombre tresses, the dressmakers had chosen a violet watered silk that shimmered and flowed under candlelight. It had the kind of real magic which can only be achieved with the right fabric and fit. In the mirror, she looked like the Fae princess she truly was, and maybe that was what made tears well in her eyes.

"Are you going to be okay with seeing your parents tonight, if they come?" I asked.

She nodded but didn't speak. I hooked my arm through hers and we marched from the king's chambers with our heads held high.

When we reached the ornate doors of the ballroom and the muted celebration inside, I leaned over to her and whispered, "Brace yourself, Brynn."

20 Brynn

Brynn was grateful for Avery's supporting arm as the doors opened onto a cacophony of sound. For her, it was not only the sounds of so many voices, or even the music playing—the din of so many spells and glamours hit her like a tidal wave of chaotic noise. Instead of an elegant entrance, she nearly collapsed under the onslaught.

Avery's gasp made Brynn aware of how hard she was gripping the human's arm and she winced in apology.

"You don't have to let go of me but your fingers were grinding my bones together," Avery whispered. "Save the bone-grinding energy for when you give your family a hug."

Brynn gave a startled laugh before she could stifle it, and heads swiveled towards her. Then the wave of curtsies and bows rolled all the way to the corners of the room—except for one couple who stood stiff above the crowd.

Brynn's mother and father, Lord and Lady Massif, had decided to put in an appearance after all. Brynn found herself walking over to them almost without her volition; if she had not known better, she would have suspected a compulsion spell. But this was only familial obligation driving her forward and leaving Avery behind.

"Daughter," her mother said in greeting. Her father merely nodded.

The fragile smile Brynn usually offered them was now more severe. "Where is the curtsy for your future queen?"

Her parents stared at her as if appalled at her joke, but when Brynn said nothing to appease them they reluctantly dipped. Barely enough to technically not to be an insult, but to still feel like one.

Brynn was not going to let them off that easily. "Do you keep in touch with Phoenix? How did he take the news?"

If she had not been looking for it, Brynn would have missed the way her parents flinched before they smiled.

"He sends his regards," her father said. "He only wishes he had more time alone with you."

His sly tone implied she likely would not have enjoyed that alone time, and that she would have deserved it.

"Alas, the king and I have something special between us," Brynn said sweetly. "It was stronger than any other obligations. I am certain you understand."

Her parents made agreeable noises but their eyes held only the same contempt they had shown for her since her carreg powers revealed themselves. Not even this dramatic change in her status could satisfy them—but instead of shame or anger, Brynn only felt relief. Now she could give herself permission to stop trying, and to let them go.

This time her own expression was sincere as she said, "Goodbye. I have other things to do and more-pleasant people to spend my time with. Enjoy the ball."

But her mother's hand on her arm stayed her. Brynn pulled away and met her mother's gaze, now filled with triumph and malice.

"You will want to see this, Daughter. Brecon has brought you a wedding gift. Is it not delightful?"

As if it had been timed with her mother's words, a fanfare played and the ballroom doors swept open again. A matched pair of unicorns trotted in, pulling a heavily glamoured cart behind them. Two figures waved regally from the velvet seat, dressed in so

many ruffles and ribbons that they were not immediately recognizable.

It was only when Riley squealed with delight
that Brynn's stomach dropped—because, of course,
there was Mara beside the child. Her beloved, also
lost in the thrall of whatever glamour held them in
its blissful grip.

"Are you not happy to see your pet humans?"
Her mother's voice dripped venom. "You always
did have a soft spot for the creatures."

Brynn clenched her fists and asked, "You knew
Brecon was planning this?"

"It was our idea," her father practically crowed.
"He knew about their existence but thought you
would see the sense of bowing to his plans on your
own—we reminded him how foolish you could be
and suggested he should think of another way to
persuade you."

Brynn turned fully to her parents and snarled,
"All my life you used my caring for others as a
cudgel to make me obey you. You made me think it
was a weakness, but it is not. What is more, I would
like to show you how much more dangerous I am to
those I do not care for."

Brynn waved a pair of guards over and was
heartened when they obeyed her immediately. Lonan must have had them standing by in case she

was in danger—*unless he was in on Brecon's plan and he anticipated she would make trouble?* Her resolve faltered momentarily, but she did not believe that of the king.

The guards bowed. "Yes, Lady Brynn?"

"Take these two to the dungeons; they have displeased me," Brynn said in her best imperious tone. "Wait—do not put them in the ground after all, down with the stones and the dark. Put them at the top of a tower, where they cannot feel the bedrock beneath them. Let the sun and the wind scour them."

Her parents exchanged glances, only just beginning to wonder if they had made a mistake.

Brynn's mother started to say, "Your brother—"

Brynn interrupted. "My brother chooses his battles. And since he has obviously underestimated me, I predict he will not be able to concern himself about you for some time. Enjoy your view from your perch."

And with a wave of her hand, she also removed the glamours from them to reveal their shabby garments and worn posture. A petty act on Brynn's part, surely, but it nonetheless made her stand taller as she strode across the ballroom.

With a worried frown creasing her brow, Avery caught up with Brynn as she was nearly to their

264

friends. Riley waved happily and skipped over to meet them.

"You won't be a fairy princess anymore, Brynn, you'll be a fairy queen!" Riley called. "And did you see my unicorns? I get to keep them!"

Brynn encouraged Mara and Riley to twirl for her, pretending to admire their dresses but actually checking them for malevolent spells. She did not put it past Brecon to put them under some sort of magical threat, since bespelling Avery had worked so well to get Lonan's cooperation.

Mara smiled as if they were all meeting in her kitchen, and not surrounded by avid Courtiers waiting for something dramatic to happen. If she was aware of how dangerous her situation was, it certainly did not show. Was there actually nothing dangerous happening?

From where he leaned against a pillar, Brecon inclined his head to his sister—making it clear the next move was hers. She raised her chin and looked him right in the eyes as she stripped away the haze of glamour around Riley and Mara.

Immediately, they both dropped to the ground and started screaming. Brynn rushed to crouch beside them, vaguely aware that Avery had done the same thing. Repeated calling of their friends' names did not break through the terrified wails. Riley and

Mara clutched at each other with eyes screwed shut, and the child started retching uncontrollably.

"What's wrong with them?" Avery asked Brynn desperately.

"I do not know," Brynn admitted. "As far as I can tell, there is no magic on them. They are not under a spell at all."

"And therein lies the problem, dear Sister," Brecon loomed over their crouching figures.

"Why are they so traumatized? What did you do?" Brynn glared at him.

"I have told you before that glamour is a kindness to humans, and I have shown these two a great mercy. You see, before I brought them here, we made a stop at the amphitheater to watch some matches."

When a horrified silence was Brynn's only response, Avery asked, "What does that mean? How did watching sports do this?"

Lonan came out of the crowd and answered, "The gladiator fights in Rome, the ones where everybody died in awful ways, were based on our own games. If Mara and Riley genuinely saw that, then...Brecon is right that a glamour is a mercy in this case."

Avery stood and buried her head in Lonan's shoulder. "Make it stop! I can't stand to see them this way."

But Brynn held up her hand. "What is the price, Brecon? Why did you bring them here?"

His grin was feral. "To remind you there are worse things than death to fear. If not for yourself, then for your pet humans. It is better for everyone if you keep your promises. All I ask is that you think of needs greater than your own. If it helps, think of your place at Lonan's side and all the good you can do as queen. In the meantime, I should return your friends to their glamoured state if you do not want them to be permanently mad."

Brynn choked, not wanting to say the words. She finally blurted, "Fine, but Lonan should glamour them. I trust him to be less heavy-handed about it."

Avery let go of Lonan so he could approach Mara and Riley. The cessation of screaming was like a balm to Brynn's aural senses. He concentrated for a moment and the two humans unfurled like flowers from their tight huddles of misery.

Mara laughed, but it seemed more like a release of tension than actual delight. She perked up when she saw Brynn, but that faded as she noticed the intricacy of her garb.

"Where are we?" she asked. "How did we get here?"

Brynn could not answer, she was so ashamed of putting them in danger. After all, she had practically confessed to Brecon that she had a new family whom she loved more than the old. Loved possibly more than herself.

Avery stepped up and answered, "You're in Faerie. I can tell you about it but I think you'd better get some rest first. Is it okay if I take them back to our—the king's chambers?"

She waited, giving Lonan, Brecon, or Brynn a chance to speak up.

"I have no objection," Brecon said. "They have served my purpose thus far. I am happy to turn over the responsibility for their welfare to someone else—keeping them fed has been tiresome."

When Brynn did not say anything, Avery turned to Lonan. Brynn listened in to their discussion of things Avery should avoid saying around the glamoured pair, to avoid triggering the memories of the arena Lonan had suppressed.

Mara was still waiting for Brynn to acknowledge them, but it was better that other Courtiers not also realize what they meant to her. So she let them turn away and follow Avery, but...the splattering of vomit from Riley glowed a deep red-purple against the white of the marble floor.

"Wait a moment," Brynn called after them.

She gently turned Riley to face her, and the same stain was all down the front of her unglamoured clothing.

"What did you eat?" Brynn demanded. Riley whimpered as Brynn's hands tightened on her arms.

Mara pulled the child away and answered, "There was a basket of fruit delivered with our meal. Something red and purple and knobbly and I wasn't sure if we should eat it, but Riley took a bite before I could stop her. She ate like three of them, is that why she threw up?"

Brynn and Lonan exchanged a look, both understanding that the child had eaten goblin fruit and would not be able to return to the human lands without wasting away. And the physical change was permanent, not merely a spell that Brynn could remove.

"What? What's wrong?" Mara asked again.

"I do not want to explain here but I will join you when I can get away from this cursed ball," Brynn told her in a low voice. "Please, go with Avery for now and we will speak later."

Mara wavered, obviously wanting to question Brynn further, but Avery herded the other humans from the ballroom. Lonan and Brynn were left with a smug Brecon, but they turned to mingle with the crowd without another word to the king's advisor.

He may have stayed a few steps ahead of Brynn with his machinations, but it was past time to remind her brother that just because he had never seen the vengeful side of her did not mean it was absent.

After all, she was an oread also and her spine was made of granite.

21 Brynn

Avery, Riley, and Mara had all fallen asleep by the time Brynn returned to the king's rooms. Their entangled forms nearly filled the king's bed, although the king himself was still at the ball. Avery stirred as Brynn let out a small noise of frustration from trying to remove her fancy dress by herself.

"Let me help," Avery said. "You may need to wear this dress again so you don't want to tear it. Why isn't Lonan with you?"

"A Nykur arrived at Court and they are trying to drink each other under the table. It could take a while, if the legends of their previous drinking contests are anything to go by."

Avery snorted as she unfastened the last in a very long row of buttons on Brynn's dress. "Yeah, I've witnessed plenty of their fratboy posturing."

Finally, Brynn was able to step out of the layers of fabric; the violet of the gown reminded her of a bruise, since she now associated it with Riley's and Mara's breakdown from seeing the truly brutal side of Faerie. Avery started to take the dress from her arms, but Brynn shook her head to say she could hang it up in the closet herself. Some time alone with her thoughts would be welcome.

As Brynn searched for a spare hanger, the dress swirled out of her hands and danced in a waltz on its own. The show finished in a flourishing curtsy and a blare of sound to her aural senses.

"Magpie?" Brynn asked softly. The wild magic answered with a bell sound and Brynn took a seat on her chaise/bed. "I am glad you are here because we need to talk."

Their conversation would have looked odd to an observer, since Brynn talked for some time and then paused before speaking again. Sometimes she nodded to herself, or shook her head, or even sighed in frustration. But eventually Brynn had learned enough that she needed to bring Avery back into the conversation.

Lonan and Avery broke off their kissing as Brynn came in the room; Lonan had rejoined them and Avery was seated in his lap on the couch. The other two still slept in the bed, so they were oblivious to anything else.

"I am glad you are here for this too, Lonan. You might be able to help," Brynn said. "I have been talking with Magpie, to ask about a theory I had."

"A theory? You talked to my wild magic without me?" Avery got up from Lonan's lap and he let out an *oof* as she accidentally elbowed him.

Brynn gave her an apologetic smile before answering. "Yes, several conversations I overheard at the ball prompted a theory. Many of the Courtiers will serve Lonan as long as it suits them, but they still wonder where—or who—the Sovereign is. A ruler upon the throne without the Sovereignty is unsettling for the Court, as well as the entire kingdom, and the constant warring serves no one's interest. Apparently, many of Lonan's backers had assumed he would claim his aunt's magic when he took the throne."

"I would have," Lonan said, "but it didn't happen. The royal magic has to make the offer and all we can do is to keep looking for likely candidates."

Brynn nodded. "I was able to ask Magpie a series of questions and as best as I can tell, the royal magic has scrutinized each person who has occupied the throne since Maeve. But it has turned away in disappointment each time, like there was some crucial trait missing. Could you tell me again exactly what Maeve said to you about how the royal magic chooses?"

Avery frowned in concentration. "Maybe Lonan remembers the exact words, but I do know she said the ruler wouldn't be either of us. And it needed to be someone who understood humans and Fae so we could co-exist, like the bumper sticker says. I don't know why Lonan would be crossed off the list, but I always assumed my lack of diplomacy took me out of the running."

"But what if it is you, Avery? What if what is lacking is your wild magic?"

Avery was already shaking her head. "No, I don't believe that. For one thing, when I had my magic, I was even more irrational. Definitely not cut out to rule anyone. Plus, how would that even work for someone to have wild magic and then add Sovereignty into the mix? I couldn't physically or mentally hold onto both when I was fighting Merlin, and shuffling the magics around is what left them marooned. I can't do that to them again."

Brynn looked to Lonan. "What do you think, my king? You were there when Avery had her wild magic. Would it be worth trying to reunite them?"

"Maybe, but not because I think it's a sure thing that she's Maeve's successor. I think she's felt the absence of her magic—and her wyvern side—a lot more than she's let on. Getting them back could make her whole again."

Avery would not meet his eyes, but her fingers subtly destroyed a tassel on the pillow next to her.

"But you think it is worth trying?" Brynn pressed him.

"Under normal circumstances I would say yes, but have you forgotten your brother's spells on Avery? The wild magic could destroy her accidentally, just by getting close."

"Magpie says it can transform the crown of thorns into something that Brecon could not bespell. Wild magic is strong enough to do it."

"But can it approach and transform it in the microsecond the spells would take to trigger? I've already said, it's not like we can experiment. It's too risky."

A silence fell as the two Fae glared at each other.

Avery spoke up, saying, "Lonan, what do you think the endgame is for us? I mean, for as long as you are the king and Brecon sees an advantage of holding me captive."

Lonan sighed. "That's just it—I know I won't be the king long-term. Either some other contender will take me out, or I'll find a way to get off the throne so we can be together."

"But that does not fit with my brother's plans," Brynn said with a bitter laugh. "Do you think he will let you walk away, and he will give you Avery back as a parting gift? No, he will do everything he can to keep you in power, because you are his own best chance at keeping his own."

"I'm still the king though, so I have some leverage over him as well." Lonan growled. "The king can compel subjects."

"Yes, but it will not stick without the Sovereignty behind it," Brynn said gently. "With the deadman's switch Brecon has added, compelling him would not buy us enough time to do anything further."

Lonan swept the food off the table in his frustration, and berries and goblin fruit rolled across the floor.

Brynn and Avery shared a look before Avery said, "I'm not happy about it either, but there's a real possibility Brecon is going to kill me no matter what. He would probably wait until you are bound to his sister with a marriage contract, but my guess is he will choose a moment with the most impact and execute me publicly. Everyone still blames me for the Shifting and he can get a lot of political mileage from throwing me under the bus."

"Hey, what's going on?" Mara asked from the bed. Lonan's tantrum had woken them at last.

"Oh, not much," Lonan said bitterly. "Brecon has us all by the short hairs and apparently we aren't doing enough about it."

"We never said that—"

Riley interrupted Brynn by asking, "Why is all the food on the floor?"

Mara sighed. "As if that will keep you from eating it, you disgusting child."

Riley only grinned at the familiar endearment, and then hopped off the bed to see what she could find to eat. Mara came to join the other grownups and they quickly caught her up with the discussion—without mentioning anything which might trigger the memories of the arena.

"I believe you all about what a bad guy Brecon is, even without my memory intact," Mara said. "And I agree you can't protect us forever, Lonan. For now, we're caught up in some power-hungry dude's web, and Riley can't even go home. She's lost nearly everything, again."

Lonan threw up his hands in surrender. "Okay, so we need to do something if we want to save Avery and to make sure Brecon can't control us. But I'm drawing the line at experimenting with Avery's Crown of Thorns—"

Avery talked over him and said, "But if my time is limited anyway, what have we got to lose? I'd rather go out fighting—"

"We have you to lose!" Lonan shouted. "I've always known you're mortal, but we were supposed to have more time together. I don't want to be king—or anything—without you."

The room went silent as Avery and Lonan locked eyes. Even Riley stopped chewing and waited to see what would happen next.

Brynn said, "Mara, Riley, do you want to change clothes? Come with me into the closet and we can pick something out."

Riley protested, but Mara urged her along and shut the closet door behind them.

Riley goggled at the rows of clothing and ran to explore every corner. "This closet is bigger than your apartment, Brynn!"

Mara raised one eyebrow at the chaise Brynn had been sleeping on, and grinned. "I did wonder where you were sleeping."

Brynn took the opportunity to reassure Mara with a hug. There were some kisses involved too, although they stopped short of jumping into a full makeout session. For now, it was enough for them to be together and listen to Riley's happy cries as she tried on fancy clothes.

"What will you do, now that Riley cannot live in your world any longer?" Brynn asked.

"My world is wherever you and Riley are, so only the place will change." But her smile was a little sad.

"That is sweet, thank you. Please know I would care for the child, if you want to return to your other life."

Mara nodded, but she seemed preoccupied. "You know, just because Avery agrees with you that we need to find a way around Brecon's spells doesn't mean it's a good idea. If anything, Avery's agreement usually means we should do the opposite of what she wants."

"Noted," said Brynn. "As angry as I am at Brecon for making you into a pawn, I do believe we have some time to figure it out. Especially if he will bide his time until Lonan and I marry."

"Marry Lonan...will you actually go through with it?"

"If it will buy all of us time, I will act as if I am engaged to the king." Brynn paused and took Mara's hand. "And if it is necessary, I will go through with it. Lonan and I both know our hearts are committed elsewhere."

"So I'll be what, your mistress?" Mara winked as she said it.

"'Kept woman' would be more apt, I think."

Before they could start up the kissing again, Riley ran over to them to show off another dress. Pale gold tulle fluttered with orange-spotted butterflies that took wing when Riley spun in place. The cloud of butterflies swirled in the air and then settled with ticklish feet on Brynn and Mara too.

They all laughed in delight, and Brynn brought one butterfly close to her face to examine it. These were obviously not natural butterflies from the human world, and yet they did not have a spell on them. With her aural senses, the creatures read as inherently magical, like a brownie or sprite. In any case, they seemed harmless.

"Do you know who would be greatly cheered by this dress?" Brynn gestured towards the main chamber with her head.

"Avery and Lonan?" Riley asked. "They would love it!"

It looked like the butterflies were exactly what Lonan and Avery needed, as their tension surrendered to a childlike delight for the colorful cloud descending upon them. Mara squeezed Brynn's hand in thanks before chasing a squealing Riley around the room.

Lonan took his crow shape and soared with the butterflies, leaving only Avery and Brynn laughing at the chaos without participating. Avery was soon covered in butterflies, as Lonan herded them in her direction.

A bell sounded to Brynn's ears, and she nodded to show Magpie she was thinking along the same lines. A plan was beginning to take shape, but she would need to gather a few things first.

"Lonan," she called, "what are the plans for today?"

He alighted on the back of the couch and answered, "Some of the Courtiers have petitioned for your help in removing curses and spells. I told them you would join me during the afternoon audience and address their needs on a case-by-case basis."

Brynn made a face and asked, "Are we free this morning then?"

Lonan cawed in a crowish laugh. "More or less. But Mara and Riley will be safer if they stay in my chambers. Anyone who means them mischief cannot enter."

Riley whined a protest but Mara nodded.

"I only need Avery's help, so that is fine," Brynn said. "We will meet up with you later, then. I am taking a nap, and then we will go."

As Brynn and Avery turned to leave, Lonan called after them, "Remember, don't take any unnecessary risks. And no experimenting."

"Yes, my king," Brynn answered with a smile.

It was not a hardship to agree, after all, when Avery had already passed one test: the butterflies had been able to land on her without triggering the Crown of Thorns. Perhaps Brecon's spells did not consider the magical beings a threat, but it was definitely something worth talking over with Magpie.

After all, wild magic who had lived all this time separate from its host was nearly a magical creature itself.

22 Avery

"Are you sure I don't have time for a bath?" I whined as I sped up to match Brynn's pace. "Or a stop at the kitchens for breakfast?"

Brynn rolled her eyes but didn't slow down. "Is that all you think about? Food and sleep?"

"Not quite all," said a voice, and I turned to see Nykur had joined us. "She also thinks about sex a lot."

I gave him a hug but then slapped his arm. "You don't know what I think about anymore, not since I let you out of my thrall."

He scoffed at me, and Brynn asked, "You know this Nykur?"

"Yeah. Can he come with us? You still haven't told me where we're going."

Brynn looked Nykur over with narrowed eyes, and he primped and posed under her gaze.

She said, "Actually, he may be able to help us get there. I do not want to say anything here, however, because Brecon has spies everywhere. Do you both trust me enough to wait until we are on our way for me to share my thoughts?"

Honestly—empathize, yes, trust not entirely. Sure, she was acting as a translator for Magpie, which was helpful, but she also had her own agenda for dealing with Brecon. If it came down to saving me or saving Mara, I had no illusions over which of us she would pick. But for now our goals were similar, so I nodded and Nykur took his lead from me.

"Do we need to let Brecon know we're leaving?" I asked. "Not that I'm itching to see him, but we don't want him to think this is a breakout attempt and hit the remote trigger."

Brynn stopped to think about my question and then reluctantly changed direction. "I suppose we had better."

The throne room was packed with partying Courtiers, like they hadn't even noticed the guests of honor—Lonan and Brynn—had left. As long as the food and drink kept coming, they could probably play out their individual dramas for all eternity. Nykur went to grab some whiskey, fuel for his car form, and Brynn and I scanned the crowd for Brecon. We didn't see him immediately so we asked around and a helpful dryad pointed us in the right direction.

Brecon's back was to us so we didn't realize who he was talking to until we were almost upon them. Brynn stiffened as she recognized her parents, but plastered a fake smile on her face.

"Brecon, I am taking Avery on a little jaunt," she said. "We will be back in plenty of time for my duties this afternoon."

Her brother turned to us with a sly gleam in his eyes. "Dear Sister, you did not greet our parents. It took some doing to track them down, only to find they claim you imprisoned them in a tower?"

Now it was my turn to freeze; Brynn hadn't mentioned this part of their encounter.

"*On* a tower, more like," she said, her grin turning a bit feral. "You have saved me the trouble of sending someone to fetch them later, so thank you, Dear Brother."

Their father started speaking in some horribly grating language, like rocks grinding and tumbling, which would have sounded threatening even if he was reciting a recipe for making taffy. *Is that oread language? It sounds like someone torturing one of those stone things you make guacamole in.*

Brecon held up a hand. "No harm done, Father. I am sure Brynn has gotten her pettiness out of her system at this point and will treat you with tolerance, if not respect, in the future."

Brynn inclined her head but spoke no promises. I knew her parents hated humans so I was tempted to draw them into conversation, but for once my sensible side won out and I just smiled at them in a human way.

"As for Avery, I am afraid she cannot leave the Court," Brecon said. "There are too many dangers out there for her, so I must insist she stay."

Brynn started to speak, but I touched her arm and drew her away where we could have a private conversation.

"Do you really need me along?" I whispered, right into her ear. "This might be a pick-your-battle moment."

"I do need you. I want a piece of wood from Merlin's tree, and I do not know the way there."

"You're in luck, because Nykur knows the way too. What do you need that wood for?"

Brynn shook her head slightly. "I have said enough and do not want to give away any more details. Will Nykur take me there on my own?"

I nodded, and we turned back to Brecon. I thought I caught his sharp gaze on us, but it was instantly replaced by his default expression of smug boredom.

"All right, I'm staying," I announced.

Brynn went to find Nykur and left me standing awkwardly with Brecon and his parents.

"Okay, so I'm going to go...not be here." I wandered off in the direction of the food, because I really hadn't had a chance to eat before Lonan turned all the food in our rooms into a floor buffet.

I loaded a plate with some of the human treats which Fae also like: cream puffs, strawberries, and even a restaurant-style veggie curry. After a traumatic experience with finding a tiny, webbed hand in my stew, I knew to avoid meat, even if it smelled and tasted like chicken. So except for the few sweets, my plate of food was healthy and vegetable-dominant.

But as I looked up and saw I was the focus of several hostile stares, I remembered the notorious Avery Flynn was only somewhat-safe at Court because Brecon claimed me as a prize-of-war. *How long before somebody decided to test Brecon's claim?*

As if I had summoned him with a thought, Brecon appeared beside me. "It may be prudent for you to retreat to the king's chambers. Shall I have more food sent up to you and the other humans there?"

I wanted to be contrary and say no, and it must have shown in my face because he said, "Please, give me this chance to show the king I am respecting our arrangement. Let me protect his interests, and mine, by keeping you safe."

I sighed and turned towards the door. A few guards bracketed me as a reminder of my protected status; groups of Fae still muttered as I passed, but they weren't so overt with their hatred.

Mara and Riley, however, welcomed me with glad cries and open arms when I got back.

"I'm so bored!" Riley said. "This is like being at the market with Mara and waiting for her to finish work."

Mara sighed. "Well, my advice is the same. Think of something fun to do—as long as you stay within these walls—or color or something."

"Oh, Lonan has some Prose Pigment around somewhere," I said. "In the closet, probably."

Riley stopped pouting long enough to ask, "What is Prose Pigment?"

"It's magical paint that makes artwork from a story you tell. And the more detailed and outlandish you are—like 'purple prose' in writing—the better the picture. You could do a mural on the closet walls, Lonan won't mind."

By the time we found the pots labeled in old-fashioned script, Riley had a story ready to burst out of her. She shoved me and Mara out of the closet so she could create her masterpiece in secret.

Meanwhile, the food had arrived and one of the covered plates revealed the lasagna that Lonan brought in especially for me. *Finally, a proper meal!* After I ate, sleepiness tried to overtake me. I fought it, since Brynn's accusation that all I thought about was food and sleep still smarted.

But Mara said I should get my rest for whatever Brynn had planned for later, and I gave in to the call of the fresh sheets on the bed. As I was drifting off, I heard a knock and voices speaking, but a pillow over my head made the noise go away.

"Avery, wake up!" Brynn's voice sounded like it was traveling through gelatin. Someone shook me, hard, and I blinked up at Nykur.

"Oh, you guys are back," I said. "How did it go?"

Then I felt stupid for asking that because as they came into focus, I could see Nykur and Brynn looked terrible. Smudges and smears discolored their torn clothes, and their exposed skin was marked with a map of burns and scratches.

"Wow, what happened? Do you want me to draw you a bath? There's room for both of you in the tub—"

"Never mind that right now," Brynn said. "Where are Mara and Riley?"

I rubbed my eyes, fighting the drowsiness that still clung to me. "Riley was in the closet working on the mural, and Mara was going to eat something. They're probably both so absorbed in painting they didn't hear you come in."

Nykur said, "We've checked. They're not anywhere in the king's chambers. Did Lonan come get them?"

Alarmed, I tried to stand but teetered on my feet. "He wouldn't have done that without waking me up. Or leaving a note—is there a note? How long have I been asleep?"

Brynn collapsed onto an ottoman. "I do not know how long you have been asleep, but it was not natural. I can see the spell fading from you, but I do not want to attempt to remove the remnants and risk endangering you. Where could they have gone?"

Panic was unraveling the sleep spell and I asked Nykur, "Can you find Lonan and discreetly see if he knows where Riley and Mara are?"

He nodded and started towards the door.

"And Nykur, maybe do something about how thrashed you look? That could give something away when we don't want it to."

My Sight twitched as a glamour fell over him, but he looked the part of a well-groomed Courtier once again. The door shut behind him and I led Brynn to the tub of always-hot water. She didn't say a word as I helped her undress, but she clutched a gnarled piece of tree root or branch so tightly I had to pry her fingers open one by one.

The water revived her enough that she waved me away, to go wait for Lonan or for word from him. First, I went into the closet to see if there was any clue as to where our friends had gone. The mural Riley had been painting stretched across the wall: mountains with dark castles bristling with gargoyles and dragons, lakes with golden ships and scaled forms bobbing in the waters, and a shining building which looked like Mrs. Dibbs's.

Riley's style was unmistakable, showcasing her fascination with magic and monsters. All except for the far end, where colors swirled uncertainly and then showed Riley and Mara brushing out the rainbow manes and tails of unicorns, like the team that had pulled their carriage.

I looked closer and in the shadows of the stable doorway, a figure watched them. The set of the head and arrogant posture reminded me of some-one. It took me a moment to realize it was Brecon, and my heart dropped to my feet.

I went back to Brynn, where she was drying off from her bath. I turned my back before speaking.

"I'm sorry to say this, but your brother may have something to do with their disappearance. He must have found a loophole in the magic which doesn't let anyone harm guests in the king's chambers—I think he lured them out with an invitation to visit the unicorns, or at least that's what it looks like from the Prose Pigment interpretation."

Brynn didn't speak, so I added, "He may only be trying to scare us, or remind us he's in charge, and they could be in the royal stables enjoying them-selves."

"We both know that is the less-likely scenario." Brynn wrapped herself in a silk dressing gown as she walked past me, back into the main room.

I paused to pick up the piece of wood she'd brought back with her, and joined her just as Lonan and Nykur came through the double doors. In spite of Brynn's words about realistic hopes, she sagged a bit when the king shook his head.

Lonan waited for the guards to close the doors before he said, "I know nothing of where Riley and

Mara could be. And Nykur says you were attacked at Merlin's tree?"

"Yes, when I went to mount Nykur for our return, a swarm of oakmen overran us. We barely fought them off."

"Do you think they acted under Brecon's orders?" Lonan asked.

"I do not know," Brynn answered. "There were no bluebells around Merlin's tree, and the oakmen did not react until I tried to take some of the tree's wood away with me. It is possible they have taken residence there and were only defending their home."

"So, no way to know if there is a connection without asking Brecon, and asking could tip him off that we're suspicious," I mused. "Do we go to the audience this afternoon as if nothing was wrong? Play it cool until we know otherwise?"

Brynn stood and said, "No, we plan as if there is a connection. I have given Brecon the benefit of the doubt so many times over the years, and he has disappointed me every time. But this is more than a disappointment—it is a deliberate, hostile move designed to remind me of my place. And I can put up with a lot, but anyone who threatens my family— my real family, not my blood—will find I am ruthless."

Damn! I hope we're real family, too? Wouldn't want to be on the wrong side of that.

"Okay, so one way or another we end this today," I said. "What's the plan?"

Nykur and Brynn exchanged a glance, and Lonan cocked his head, birdlike. *Are they all in on it except me?*

"The plan is for you to not know about the plan," Lonan confirmed. "It's not you we don't trust—it's Brecon. If we want to get out from under his thumb, he can't know what we're doing."

"And you think he's using me to eavesdrop or something?" I asked.

"We don't know," Nykur said with a shrug. "We'll only get one chance at this, though."

I sighed. "Fine. I'll go take a bath or something and let you all talk in here."

A hot bath is not nearly so relaxing when you know you're missing out on exciting plans. I was just as done with Brecon and his using me as Brynn was, but it had always been difficult for me to let go of control. Or to be patient. I lasted about an hour before I had enough and went to rejoin the others. Only Brynn was there, looking like she was about to fall asleep.

"Where's everyone else?"

She started awake and answered, "Nykur went to see if he could find any rumors of Riley's and Mara's whereabouts, and Lonan is—well, he's tracking down how that sleep spell got to you."

"I got sleepy after eating the lasagna, so I'm guessing it was in there."

Brynn nodded. "Lonan suspected that as well. When he finds who added it to your food, they will pay a hard price for their betrayal. A king needs to be able to trust the kitchen staff absolutely."

"But Brecon is behind it, right? We already know that."

"He may have ordered it, but he would have had someone else do it."

"Yeah, your brother doesn't like to get his own hands dirty," I said. "But I wish Lonan didn't have to, either. I feel like it's changing him, having to make these rulings and punishments. Plus, he's not even the Sovereign, so he doesn't have the royal magic to guide him. That's a lot of pressure, and he basically signed up to save me. Lot of good it did."

"Can you not say you would do the same for him?"

"Are you asking in a general 'you love each other' way, or because you still think I might be the one on the throne if I had my wild magic?"

Brynn laughed. "They are not mutually exclusive, as I believe the phrase goes? In any case, we should get dressed for the audience. We are still expected to appear, however difficult it will be not to slap Brecon on sight."

I sighed and followed Brynn into the closet, where two dresses were waiting. One with a skirt painted like a watercolor of an iris flower, and the butterfly dress Riley had been modeling before.

"Dibs on the flower dress!" I blurted.

But Brynn shook her head and said, "Lonan is expecting to see you in the butterflies. We thought it would be so cheerful for when we find Riley and Mara."

"But isn't an audience with the king—and future queen—meant to be serious? Butterflies feel too frivolous."

Brynn arched an eyebrow. "I would not have guessed you cared so much for the opinion of the Court."

Ha, as if I don't know a dare when I hear one. But if Brynn was insisting, maybe it was part of the Plan with a capital P.

"Fine." Orange wings swirled around me as I stepped into the dress and Brynn waited to fit it to me. "Make sure not to accidentally stab me or the butterflies when you pin me up."

The butterflies made it through the process without a stabbing, but I didn't. One pin scratched my arm and a line of blood welled up. The butterflies immediately alighted for a sip of the red juice. *Because even magical butterflies feed on blood in Faerie, yay.*

23 Brynn

When Brynn and Avery entered the throne room, King Lonan had already been hearing requests from his subjects long enough for boredom to set in. Or rather, the Court was bored, but the king vibrated subtly like a guitar string under tension. Mara and Riley were not there, although some small part of Brynn had hoped they would be waiting, happy and unharmed.

Lonan stood and welcomed both Brynn and Avery onto the dais. From its height, Brynn saw her brother circulating among the Courtiers, probably accepting bribes and calling in favors. His network of spies would have delivered secrets and tidbits for him to use to cajole—or extort—his targets.

Brynn had a sudden thought that Brecon's strategy of keeping tabs on so many details was not unlike what Mara did, although Mara used her network for good. The contrast of her efforts to match customers with things they needed (or did not yet know they needed), and Brecon's need to control others through their weaknesses only made it more obvious Brecon had chosen power over kindness.

It was a waste of his talents, but Brynn knew there could be no convincing him otherwise. With that realization, Brynn let go of her heart's last tie to the loving younger brother she had once known. The Fae he had become was no brother of hers, and the parents who had only offered her contempt and abuse could go dwindle into sand for all she cared.

"My dear?" Lonan's voice caught her attention and Brynn realized everyone was staring at her, waiting for her to take Lonan's hand.

She smiled and nodded, gracefully taking her seat. The next Fae stepped forward and she listened as they spoke of a grievance with a neighbor. It was a simple dispute over boundaries, so her special talents were not needed.

But the Fae who followed were obviously under a curse. A couple and their young child groveled before the dais, shedding patches of putrid flesh and dripping an ichor that sizzled as it hit the marble.

"What is this?" Brynn asked.

"Please, Your Highness, our child crossed a Tiddy Mun and he has cursed us, as you see. Can you do aught?"

Where she stood behind the thrones, Avery snorted and whispered, "Tiddy Mun."

"Tiddy Mun has some powerful curses," Brynn said for Avery's benefit. "But yes, I can help."

She leaned forward, although of course that actually did nothing to help Brynn "hear" better with her aural senses. The sound of the curse was a trombone with warped notes burbling through tar. It bubbled and squeaked in time with the eruptions of the afflicted family's boils and carbuncles, nearly as miserable to hear as it was to experience.

Brecon had instructed her to display some showmanship when using her powers; the Court appreciated a flair for drama. But not only was it not Brynn's style, somewhere in this queue of complainants was the next step in their plan: the catalyst which would make it possible to regain control over their lives, and that of their loved ones.

So, Brynn simply waved her hand and the curse sloughed off like another layer of ruined skin. The family stood before her unharmed, and dressed in servant's garb. They could have been any indentured Fae worker, like the ones who had labored at her own family's castle.

Their gratitude was echoed by cries of amazement from the Courtiers. But for every delighted face, there were two scowling visages: not everyone appreciated that curses and spells could be undone so easily by the Fae who could soon be occupying the queen's throne permanently. They did not like the possibility that their own magic was meaningless in the face of such power.

The rest of the cursed subjects now pushed their way to the front of the line, crowding the dais so much that the Host stepped in to sort them out. This would not do, since Lonan's "plant" in the crowd needed to be able to approach the dais.

Brynn worked as fast as she could, even removing a few curses from unknowing victims in the corners of the throne room. Startled cries mingled with joyous ones, until the line was only the usual complaints and requests again. Lonan handled those with dispatch, and Brynn could tell he too was getting impatient. Being on alert for so long was taking a toll on them.

Finally, a strange character approached the dais. Dressed in feathers of black and white, the Fae bowed and introduced himself.

"My king, I am your cousin, Patchelthwaite. If you are in need of entertainment, please call upon me."

Lonan cocked his head. "A cousin, eh? Corbin?"

Brynn sat up straighter, holding her breath as she waited to see if this was the Fae they were waiting for.

"The finest of corbin, indeed," Patchelthwaite confirmed.

As he bowed, countless birds burst from his sleeves. A murmuration of blackbirds wheeling and darting, jackdaws clacking their bone-pale beaks, grackles diving at laughing Courtiers, and magpies landing on finely dressed Fae so they could peck at shining jewels. It was the kind of chaos that corbins love, and the king was no exception.

Lonan coaxed some of the birds to take tidbits from his fingers and they flocked to the dais, recognizing an easy mark when they saw one. Avery joined in the laughter as a few birds darted around her, trying to catch the butterflies on the wing.

Brynn held her breath and watched Avery from the corner of her eye; it would not do to pay too close attention and stoke Brecon's suspicions.

There it was—a magpie, more self-possessed than the others. It landed on Avery's shoulder, causing a ripple in the orange butterfly wings as they made room for another passenger. The magpie cocked its head, one shining eye trained on the strange collar Avery wore.

As it leaned forward to peck at the Crown of Thorns, Brynn simultaneously leapt to her feet. Time seemed to slow down, so she was able to see it all unfold: the magpie touched the deadly collar and then, a twining ring of ivy circled Avery's neck instead. Avery reached for it wonderingly, but the magpie was already snatching it into flight.

Brecon's head turned just in time to watch the magpie—with its prize—fly straight into one of the everlasting candle flames. With a horrid stench, the bird and transformed Crown of Thorns blazed into ash, freeing Magpie from the shell which had let it get close enough to perform its trick.

Simultaneously, Brynn leapt towards Avery, her aural senses already separating the notes of Merlin's curse and snuffing them out. Avery's wild magic rushed into the void left by the spell. The moment when Avery could feel her wild magic—Magpie—was obvious, as wonder-joy-recognition-rapture cycled through her expression.

And then, it was no longer a human girl standing there—a burly, scaled body split the tulle dress and the wyvern let out a bloodthirsty roar. The possibility that Avery would become her wyvern self once reunited with her wild magic had been discussed during the plan, but Brynn had not expected it to happen so quickly or completely.

Brynn crouched down and covered her ears from Avery's triumphant bellow, and felt a hand tugging on her dress. Seeing that Lonan was trying to pull her away, she crab walked to the edge of the dais and slid to the polished marble floor.

Lonan's steps hesitated only a little as he approached the wyvern, who was now hunched in a defensive stance. The Host started to come to the king's aid, but he waved them off as wyvern-Avery lowered her head in a submissive bow.

Brynn took her eyes off the king and swept the crowd for Brecon. Her brother shoved his way through the panicked crowd, and Brynn could sense him gathering magic. She reached out and sapped the coiling spell faster than he could form it.

He shouted something at her and shook his fist, but he soon had something worse to worry about. Avery had spotted him and she bared her teeth in a snarl. Lonan made a grab for one of her four arms, but her wings were already unfurling and the king had to drop to the floor to avoid being struck.

Avery was on Brecon in a moment, knocking him down and savaging his forearm as he tried to protect his face. Brynn could not help feeling some satisfaction at seeing her arrogant brother brought low, but killing him might mean the whereabouts of Mara and Riley would disappear also.

Now it was Brynn's turn to urge Lonan along, as he was the only one who might get through to Avery in her current state. The wyvern growled at them as they approached, but Lonan spoke in a soft voice, even whispering a word which may have been her Name. Finally, Avery sat back on her muscled haunches and the light of intelligence showed in her eyes again.

"It's your call, Brynn," she said. "Do you want him dead or alive?"

"Alive. We need him to tell us what he did with Mara and Riley."

"Well?" Avery asked, resting a claw against his neck.

"I want a guarantee of my safety," Brecon said, with some of his old bravado. "From King Lonan."

"I will not let Avery kill you, if you are quick enough to answer," Lonan drawled.

"Not Avery, not anyone. I will leave this Court alive, King of the Corbins."

Lonan rolled his eyes, but agreed to the terms.

Brecon looked at his sister as he answered, "They are on the tower. The one where you put Mother and Father. I thought it only fair."

Byrnn was about to call a guard to fetch them when Avery took flight.

"I can get them faster."

Brecon started to sit up, but at a gesture from the king, the Host surrounded him with weapons drawn. A sneer lifted Brecon's lip, but it fell into an expression of stark terror as one of the guards pulled out a pair of shackles and placed them on Brecon's wrists. Once they clicked shut, his ability to perform any spells, and his glamour, fell away.

Brynn was tempted to show him some pettiness by delivering a hard kick while he was helpless, but a whoosh of wings caught her attention. It was Avery, back already, and with two still forms cradled in her arms. She hovered for a moment, frowning down at the milling crowd, like chickens running for cover from a falcon.

The only clear spot was the dais, as the Host had formed a cordon around it and the king. Avery swooped down to carefully place Riley in one throne and Mara in the other. The two figures slumped in the oversized thrones, heads lolling and their faces covered by their windswept hair.

Brynn was already running back to join them, but the Host held her back until Lonan waved her through. Now her steps slowed; as long as Brynn had not touched them yet, to see if their flesh felt as cold as it looked, then there was the possibility they were still alive. Merely unconscious from their ordeal on an exposed tower top.

But Avery was already checking Riley for a pulse, with her now-human fingers. The fact she was also nude did not even get a second look, here at Court. Nonetheless, one of the Host draped the remains of her gown over her.

Avery looked up and smiled. "Riley's alive. I think she's chilled through—it was pretty rough up there for a human."

Brynn hurried over to Mara's side and perched on the throne's arm, bracing herself for what she might find. She twined her hands with Mara's, trying to warm them with her own body heat.

Mara's fingers twitched and then curled against Brynn's, who gripped harder so Mara could not let go. Mara's eyelids fluttered before she gazed back at Brynn.

"I am so glad you are all right—" Brynn started to say, but she trailed off as she noticed a strange phenomenon. It was as if all sound in the vast room ceased. Not muffled or warped, but just absent. Even her aural senses were silent and still, something Brynn had never experienced before in her life.

Alarmed, she looked around and it seemed no one else had noticed anything odd—because they were frozen in whatever position they had been in when this bubble rose up: Riley and Avery in mid-conversation, and Brynn's parents in mid-argument with the king's guards.

"What's happening?" Mara whispered. Somehow, whispering made sense in the soundless bubble.

"I am not sure," Brynn answered, wrapping Mara in a hug. "We could be under attack or a spell somehow, but it does not feel like that."

"No—it feels safe, doesn't it?"

Brynn could only nod in agreement as she stretched her hearing and her aural senses to pick up anything, any sound at all. There was only a faint scratching sensation, as if there was a sound barely under the threshold of her ability to hear it. Then it strengthened to whispers, uncountable voices overlapping and overwhelming each other.

Strangely though, it was not unpleasant. More like an incredibly complex piece of poetry, spoken by thousands—perhaps millions—of voices at once.

"What is that?" Mara was whispering again, and her hand squeezed Brynn's painfully.

"You can hear it? Then it is not some glitch in my carreg magic."

"I can hear it...it's like the volume is slowly being turned up, to give us time to get used to it."

They both paused to listen.

"I think you are right," Brynn said.

She closed her eyes, the better to try to sort out the sounds. The volume reached a comfortable level and plateaued there, before Brynn started seeing flashes through her eyelids. Startled, she opened her eyes and saw a network of lines was laid over everything, and the flashes were traveling along them.

Mara's gasp made her look down at their joined hands, and all the lines seemed to meet at a pulsing orb nestled between their palms. The throbbing light was nearly too bright to look at and as Brynn's alarm heightened, the pulsating grew faster.

"Hey, it's all right," Mara said. And somehow, Brynn could feel her reaching through their connection and helping her to feel calmer. To feel loved.

"How are you doing that?" Brynn breathed. "You are human."

"I am, but I think maybe...maybe, I'm also the Sovereign. Or, at least half—I think *we* are the rulers of Faerie now, and this is the royal magic."

"That is...unlikely." But even as she said it, Brynn knew it too. "How did you know, before I did?"

"Because of him." With her free hand, Mara pointed behind Brynn.

For a moment, she was too frightened to turn around, but again the comfort flowed from Mara into her and she managed it.

24 Brynn

Standing stock-still on the dais was a Wild Huntsman, as if he had been there the entire time and was waiting for them to notice. Without his horse, he should have been less intimidating—smaller, even.

But somehow, he was even more disturbing. Brynn squinted and realized it was because he wore an aura of energy, like a cloak of wavelengths in different colors, completely different from the energy flowing through the interconnected lines. Like he was in a dimension apart from Faerie, yet also in the space with Brynn and Mara.

"That's the one who Avery calls Silent Knob," Mara whispered. "If the Huntsmen have a leader, it's him. What does he want?"

The answer came from the Huntsman himself, in a wordless series of images.

"Are you getting that?" Mara asked.

"He seems to be confirming the royal magic is indeed favoring us as rulers, but it is still up to us whether to accept or not. And the offer is for both of us, or neither."

"Your connection to him must be better than mine," Mara said. "I'm just getting...like, emotions, without any details. What happens if we don't want to be in charge?"

A pause as Brynn took in the reply. "The magic setting us apart will dissipate and return us to the Court without any the wiser. And the royal magic will continue to look for another match, however long that may take."

"Do we have time to think about it?"

Brynn did not need to relay that one, as the royal magic itself seemed to chuckle in answer. It may as well have said, "Yes, this bubble is exactly that: a gift of time so you can consider the offer without outside interference."

Silent Knob went back to being, well, silent. Brynn and Mara were left to discuss their pending coronation—or return to normalcy.

"Tell me what you are thinking," Brynn said. She leaned into Mara, somehow needing more of themselves in contact to better communicate.

Mara sighed. "I'm thinking that I don't know if I even want anything to do with the Court. Out of all the Fae I've been around, these seem to only want power, revenge, dominance—and they treat humans like toys. Trash, even."

Brynn could not argue with that. She waited to see if the Huntsman or royal magic had any rebuttal, but they did not. It seemed she and Mara would have to sort this out themselves.

"I will say that I believe those traits you mentioned are being amplified *because* of the lack of a true ruler," Brynn countered. "Through the network of the Sovereignty, the ruler has an immense influence on their subjects as well. Not to control them directly, but perhaps we can offer an environment where they could see different possibilities. To live better lives, perhaps."

Mara's lips twisted into a wry smile. "And on the flip side, if it's not us then someone worse could end up on the throne. Someone who is not concerned with how humans are treated—or with how humans and Fae treat each other."

Brynn thought back to Queen Maeve's description which had sent Avery and Lonan on their quest. "I do think the royal magic would continue to look for a candidate who will try to balance the needs of humans and Fae—whether that would be another pairing like us or a person who merely has ties to both worlds, it is impossible for me to say.

"You know I have not had the best experience with my family and other Fae, who reject me because of my carreg magic. But since I have been in the wider world, I have seen further sides of my people and the humans. We are all more flawed, but also more kind, than I expected—more alike. What if you and I can help them realize that?"

Mara unconsciously rubbed her arms, covered with scratches from her time on the tower. Brynn did not need the dread thrumming through the royal magic to know Mara was not convinced. Brynn, however, saw this opportunity as a way to heal the Court and Spellmeet, and perhaps send ripples of peace into the rest of the worlds. It would only happen if her partner could also see the same opportunity.

Already figuring out how to interpret the root of Mara's feelings, Brynn changed her tack. "I have seen you with old Mrs. Fumagalli at the market. She is rude to everyone—except the hen she pushes in that stroller—and other sellers refuse to deal with her. She is still nothing but surly to you, even after all the help you have given her over the years. So why do you put up with her?"

Mara smiled. "It's because she dotes on that chicken. It means she can't be all bad, if she has love for that feather-duster."

"Being nice to a chicken but completely awful to everyone else balances each other out?"

Brynn's challenge seemed to be pushing Mara into serious topics, a place where she was never comfortable. So Mara chuckled and gave Brynn a half-flippant answer.

"It's not like I let her abuse me. She's learned that pitching a fit isn't the way to get my attention, or to get my above-and-beyond level of service. The other vendors mostly give in to make her go away, so she might get some free tomatoes but she's still alone when she eats them."

Brynn waited for more. Mara heaved a sigh and the opening gates of her emotions freed up the blocked lines of power running from her to Brynn.

"I don't help Nora Fumagalli because she deserves it for her own sake," Mara admitted. "I take care of her for my sake—because I don't want to be that person who sees an old lady struggling, and who then looks the other way. I want to be the one to reach out a hand—even if there's a chance it'll get bitten. Or pecked at, I guess." A small smile snuck out.

Brynn squeezed Mara's hands and sent her a burst of love and approval. "Faerie is struggling now, and so is Spellmeet, with its people and places admixed without regard for past grievances. Someone needs to shape and guide the future of both worlds."

"And you think that's us? It took me weeks to let you into my life, partly because I have seen so many human-Fae relationships go wrong. I didn't want to find out you were secretly like the others, and going to throw me away when you were finished playing house. Does that sound like a ruler who's going to give Fae a fair shake?"

Brynn kissed her on the cheek. "Despite your fears, you were open-minded enough to recognize I was not going to treat you so shabbily, once you got to know me. You can do so again, especially with me at your side and the Sovereignty connecting us to all the lives in our hands."

Mara looked like she wanted to argue further, but their connection meant she could see Brynn's sincerity was absolute. "You didn't want to be queen before, Brynn, so why have you changed your mind?"

"That was when I would have been a puppet queen. I would have needed to fight Brecon—and perhaps Lonan—for any hint of autonomy. That's not how it would be with us as Sovereigns."

A frisson of hope shivered down the power lines. "You really think we can do this? You really *want* to do this?"

"I have learned that I get an immense satisfaction from helping others, whether they are Fae or human. As you said, it is not always about whether the recipient deserves our help, but also about making a choice that we want to make a difference, and acting on that decision. I was drawn to you because I recognized the same desire. Are you saying I was mistaken?"

"No, but...what if we're not enough? Even if we're trying to make things better, how do we keep our sights on what is 'better' for our subjects?"

Brynn lifted their joined hands, bringing the networking lines into Mara's line of sight. "I believe that is where the Sovereignty will help us. And our own growing relationship."

When Mara sighed and nodded, Brynn knew she had decided they would accept the Sovereignty. But sometimes magic needed a more obvious confirmation, like saying it aloud.

Brynn got on one knee and gazed up at Mara, still sitting on the throne. "Mara, will you do me—and the royal magic—the honor of joining with us? In making a commitment for life, and for better lives."

"I will. Or should I say I do? Either way, it's yes."

Brynn perched on the throne's arm again, the better for them to seal the accord with a kiss. The magic surged around them, through them, making them two people working in sync—but with the payoff that they also felt such a deep harmony. A balm for carreg senses, and also for a human with such pain and loss in her past. The two of them, together, were home.

"You know," Brynn mused, "this is the last time we may get a peaceful time together, just the two of us."

The Huntsman had disappeared at the moment when they had "officially" accepted, so they were indeed alone. They did not rush as they explored each other's bodies, and when they were tired, they asked questions they had not thought to ask before. And got to know each other on a completely different level, as they communicated through the royal magic's web also.

The only thing which would have made the interlude better was wonderful food and drink to share. Time may not be passing outside their bubble, but inside it the time was now being marked with growling stomachs. Mara stood up to stretch and when Brynn did the same, they knew it was time to rejoin the worlds. After a check to make sure their clothes were back in place, they joined hands and faced out to the Court.

"We're ready—" Mara started to say, but with a shimmer and an audible *pop!*, the domed ceiling over their safe space disappeared.

After its absence, the sound and chaos hit them so hard that they both stumbled backwards. The overwhelm almost made them fall to their knees, but they were both too stubborn for that—and also highly aware they would need to show united strength in their new roles.

Flashes of emotion from their subjects sped along the network of royal magic, and Brynn and Mara knew people were noticing something was different at Court. Then, like a field of sunflowers, the faces of the Courtiers all turned to the dais and their new Sovereigns.

The talking faded to whispered murmurs, and after only a glance between them, Brynn and Mara sent emotions down the pipeline: safety, security, joy, togetherness, contentment. What was more, they got such a sense of relief coming back to them. A collective sigh sounded and then the Courtiers dropped into curtsies and bows. Avery, Lonan, and Riley did not bow right away, but that seemed to be because they were so stunned. As soon as they recovered, they too bent in respect.

A disturbance started in the crowd, as well as in the royal magic's network, as three Fae pushed through the ranks. Brecon still had on his magic-depleting shackles, but had no trouble making his voice heard without an amplification spell.

"Ah, Dear Sister, you have taken your rightful place at last. Allow me to take your human to wait for you in your chambers, and then you may address your Fae subjects without distraction."

Mara barked a laugh at Brecon's attempts to take charge.

Brynn smiled too and said, "Take another look, Dear Brother."

She raised her hand where it was still entwined with Mara's and limned with Sovereignty. As he realized they were joined to each other and the magic, his charming smile faltered.

"The Sovereignty has settled on a *human*?" Brynn's mother spat out. "But it is a Fae magic."

"Not purely Fae any longer," Brynn replied.

Mara added, "The magic is now a blending of human and Fae gifts, just as our Court will now reflect our Fae and human subjects."

A handful of gasps sounded in the room, but were quickly stifled. Only Brynn's family was still showing outright hostility to the idea that they would soon be sharing privileges with humans. Brecon had dropped his charming façade and fought against his shackles, only to give up and glare at his new monarchs.

"That human will never last and you would be better off sharing your throne with someone like me," he snapped. "Humans are too vulnerable, as I myself have proven time and again."

Brynn's smile now more closely resembled a snarl. "You would threaten one of your queens?"

A smirk. "If not her, then some other human she loves. It is easily done."

Brynn and Mara did not need to glance at each other as they conferred; they were quickly getting used to using their shared magic as a conduit for secret conversations, too.

Brynn said aloud, "In the days to come, we will put binding, magical laws in place, but all of you should know: any threats and hostile actions against humans by the Fae will not be tolerated. Any humans currently serving in Fae households against their will must be freed. We need to work together, not against each other."

"And if we refuse?" Brecon asked with a sneer.

Brynn held up a hand. "I was planning on giving you a chance at a trial, Brother, but since you persist in your species-ist ways, you may be an example instead.

"One thing which may interest you—and any others who are secretly harboring crimes against humanity—is that the Sovereignty is protecting Mara, as it has with countless generations of rulers before. Acting against her will have swift and brutal consequences."

"Brutal?" Brecon scoffed. "You are far too soft. Will you order me to read bedtime stories to human children? Or make me believe I love those stinking animals?"

Brynn shrugged. "You may choose to do those things on your own, but I have a different punishment in mind. It may surprise you that I am still learning the ways royal magic and carreg magic work together. For example, I only a moment ago realized I could do this."

At the wave of her hand, Brecon howled in pain and collapsed to his knees. It was not obvious what was happening to him, but it was certainly agonizing. The screams went on as his parents stepped back in horror. Finally, he lay on the floor shuddering and the only sound was the *click* of his wrist shackles unfastening and falling away, since they were no longer needed.

Brynn and Mara sat in their thrones and waited for him to collect himself. Brecon got to his knees and then stood on trembling legs.

"What did you do? Why do I feel so...weak and strange?"

Brynn looked to Mara. "Do you want to tell him or shall I?"

Mara's grin was feral. "You tell him."

"All right. Dear Brecon, my carreg magic still operates much like it did before it joined with the royal magic, but it also has some new...superpowers, if you will. I have stripped away all of your magic, cancelling it as quickly as it flowed from your body. You now have no more magic in you than a simple rock does, nor the capacity to regain it."

Cries of horror rippled through the Court as Brecon raised his hands and stared at them, straining to call up any iota of magic. But nothing answered his call, not even his...

"Mountain," he gasped. "Where is my tie to my mountain?"

"I am sorry to say that is gone also, as I could not leave you the ability to recharge at your mountain. But do not worry, you can survive without it now, so you will not die or dwindle from the lack of your connection to your former anchor."

Brecon looked as if he would vomit at this news. Their father cried out, "He cannot be an oread without his mountain. Without it, he is nothing."

Mara laughed. "Not quite nothing. In fact, without his native magic and his mountain, Brecon is now basically a human."

Her expression dared Brecon, or Lord and Lady Massif, to say being human was worse than nothing. They obviously wanted to, but they were also getting an inkling that their soft Brynn was perhaps more ruthless and vengeful than they had expected.

"Whatever you do, don't eat the goblin fruit now, Uncle Brecon." Riley's voice filled the silence. "We don't wanna be stuck with you here in Faerie."

Riley's comment startled a bark of laughter out of Avery, and as if that was a signal, the Courtiers started talking amongst themselves again. Brecon and his parents were now circled by the backs of their former friends, as they turned away from the horrifying spectacle of a Fae reduced to a human's status. And even Lord and Lady Massif sidled towards escape.

Riley skipped up the steps to join the queens. "So, are you my mom now too, Brynn?"

She smiled and answered, "I suppose I am. Is that okay?"

The child shrugged. "I guess the only thing better than having a real Fairy princess for a stepmom is having two queens as my moms. What's next?"

"We will need to figure that out together," Mara said.

"As a family," Brynn added with a hug to her most-precious humans.

EPILOGUE Avery

If I truly deserved any kind of reward for saving the worlds during the Shifting, I was happy that reward turned out to be no longer having to save the worlds. Now we had two Sovereigns for that, working in harmony due to their connection to each other, and both worlds, via the royal magic.

And if their first official act was anything to go by, humans and Fae were headed to a more equal existence: the arena where humans, Fae, and creatures annihilated each other for sport—gone, by royal decree. Plus, humans previously doomed to unwilling servitude were now free from their glamours or geises and able to choose their own paths. Surprisingly, many of them opted to stay employed in Faerie or Spellmeet—for proper wages, of course.

Riley didn't have a choice about staying—since she'd had the Goblin Fruit, human food couldn't sustain her anymore. Sure, she could go back to the human world but she'd be starving the entire time. Riley and I weren't built to go hungry for long. But if any human was excited for life in Faerie, it was Riley and her wishes to live with unicorns and magic. Her moms will make sure she does just fine.

As for Lonan and I, we were cleared of any wrongdoing and the Majesties awarded us medals instead. And once we told Queen Brynn about Shady Grove, she and Queen Mara sent funding and workers to help support Mrs. Shore, and to get her advice on setting up similar care homes for humans and Fae left damaged by the aftermath of the Border's collapse.

That went so well that Lonan and I were out of a job—and let's face it, there were others more patient and better-suited to it than a restored wild magic girl and her corbin companion. Once we'd trained some newbies, we could hit the road and travel as we pleased.

Sure, there was still a certain amount of notoriety for the ex-king and his concubine, but at least it wasn't the kind that got us pitchforked on sight. It was the kind of notoriety that got Lonan offered endless pints wherever we stayed, though, so good thing his legendary alcohol tolerance was real.

On the itinerary were stops at my mom's and my dad's, now that it was safe for them to be associated with me again. And we traveled with the Wild Hunt for a few nights, so Lonan could get some of his dark Fae out of his system. He and the Huntsmen chased villains while Daniel and I caught each other up with our lives and our plans.

I was genuinely glad to hear he even had plans, instead of being stuck in the trauma of all that had happened to him in Faerie before. He promised to look up Mrs. Shore if the dark thoughts over-whelmed him again, and we parted on better terms. Maybe Lonan and I can get a dog like Bobbin, once we're more settled.

Not yet though, because I needed all my extra at-tention for relearning to coexist with my wild mag-ic. When I'd had it before, it was a voice in my head—a strongly opinionated voice, yeah, but still a part of me. But after living "wild" for so long, Mag-pie had evolved its own personality and was now more like another, separate mind ricocheting inside my brain.

Lonan said that's the sort of thing that can drive people mad, but how could we tell in my case? *Hardy har har.*

Magpie took every opportunity to remind me how clever it was to think up that plan to save me. See, once Magpie and Brynn realized smaller magical creatures could get close to me without the COT detonating, they only needed to come up with a magical creature who could hide Magpie inside it. Like a Trojan horse-fly or something.

When Magpie had been on walkabout after the Shifting, it had swung by Merlin's tree and discovered the oak was imbued with his wild magic, so much so that it was particularly receptive to Magpie's magic. After Brynn fetched a piece of it, Nykur carved it into a crude bird shape to act as a vessel.

Once the Magpie-in-a-magpie got close enough to me to neutralize the Crown of Thorns and then throw itself into the candle flame, there was only a millisecond for Brynn to strip away the curse and to allow Magpie to leap back into me. Magpie did, and here we are.

Good thing Lonan is a corbin and understands about an extra passenger in my body—he says he always knew he would talk me into a throuple. And lucky me, Magpie and Lonan have similar senses of humor, so I can look forward to a lifetime of "jokes" like that.

Brace yourself, Avery.

ACKNOWLEDGMENTS

I wanted this book to come out shortly after Merlin's Stronghold, but the gods had other ideas. First there came the Pestilence, which upended everyone's lives.

Then for me specifically, there came the personal pestilence of cancer. Thanks are due to those who helped me through it, including my husband, my friends (especially the SCBWI friends and Fearless 15ers who cheered me on), the medical team, and Triumph Cancer Foundation.

Editors Bethany Hensel and Amy Rogers stepped up to help me get Spellmeet ready for readers, and Kelley York of Sleepy Fox Studio pulled another outstanding cover out of her magic hat.

ABOUT THE AUTHOR

Angelica R. Jackson is a writer, artist, and avid naturalist living in the Sierra foothills of California. She is currently owned by a Miniature Pinscher/Nibblonian mix named Finn.

She is the author of the award-winning Faerie Crossed young adult urban fantasy series, and her photos are collected in Capturing The Castle: Images of Preston Castle (2006-2016). Her artwork also appears on her Charming Corby Jewelry, a line of handmade cabochon pieces.